"Promise you won't say anything. It's very important to me. If Kevin is really interested in me, he'll ask me out again on a real date. In the meantime, I don't want Liz plotting anything. If she thinks Kevin only walks me to class, she won't pay attention to us."

Kathy couldn't let Marcie know the depth of her feelings for Kevin because she was uncertain of them herself. She had never felt this way before about a boy, but she had not had much experience. Maybe this was just puppy love...

Caprice Romances from Tempo Books

SMALL TOWN SUMMER by *Carol Ellis*
DANCE WITH A STRANGER by *Elizabeth Van Steenwyk*
TERRI'S DREAM by *Margaret Garland*
BEFORE LOVE by *Gloria D. Miklowitz*
PINK AND WHITE STRIPED SUMMER by *Hazel Krantz*
SUNRISE by *G. C. Wisler*
THREE'S A CROWD by *Nola Carlson*
A SPECIAL LOVE by *Harriette S. Abels*
SOMEONE FOR SARA by *Judith Enderle*
S.W.A.K. SEALED WITH A KISS by *Judith Enderle*
CARRIE LOVES SUPERMAN by *Gloria D. Miklowitz*
PROGRAMMED FOR LOVE by *Judith Enderle*
A NEW LOVE FOR LISA by *Harriette S. Abels*
WISH FOR TOMORROW by *Pam Ketter*
THE BOY NEXT DOOR by *Wendy Storm*
A HAT FULL OF LOVE by *Barbara Steiner*
TWO LOVES FOR TINA by *Maurine Miller*
LOVE IN FOCUS by *Margaret Meacham*
DO YOU REALLY LOVE ME? by *Jeanne R. Lenz*
A BICYCLE BUILT FOR TWO by *Susan Shaw*
A NEW FACE IN THE MIRROR by *Nola Carlson*
TOO YOUNG TO KNOW by *Margaret M. Scariano*
SURFER GIRL by *Francess Lin Lantz*
LOVE BYTE by *Helane Zeiger*
WHEN WISHES COME TRUE by *Judith Enderle*
HEARTBREAKER by *Terry Hunter*
LOVE NOTES by *Leah Dionne*
NEVER SAY NEVER by *Ann Boyle*
THE HIDDEN HEART by *Barbara Ball*
TOMMY LOVES TINA by *Janet Quin-Harkin*
HEARTWAVES by *Deborah Kent*
STARDUST SUMMER by *Pam Ketter*
LAST KISS IN APRIL by *N. R. Selden*
SING A SONG OF LOVE by *Judith Enderle*
ROCK 'N' ROLL ROMANCE by *Francess Lin Lantz*
SPRING DREAMS by *Nola Carlson*
CHANGE OF HEART by *Charlotte White*
PRESCRIPTION FOR LOVE by *Judie Rae*
CUPID CONFUSION by *Harriette S. Abels*
WILL I SEE YOU NEXT SUMMER? by *Judith Enderle*
SENIOR BLUES by *Francess Lin Lantz*
NEW KID IN TOWN by *Jean Thesman*

A CAPRICE ROMANCE

New Kid in Town
Jean Thesman

TEMPO BOOKS, NEW YORK

NEW KID IN TOWN

A Tempo Book/published by arrangement with
the author

PRINTING HISTORY
Tempo Original/August 1984

ISBN: 0-441-57154-9

Tempo Books are published by The Berkley Publishing Group,
200 Madison Avenue, New York, New York 10016.
Tempo Books are registered in the United States Patent Office.
PRINTED IN THE UNITED STATES OF AMERICA

New Kid in Town

Chapter 1

Nervously, Kathleen Price ran slender fingers through her damp blond hair, coaxing curls down on her forehead. The large mirror beside the front door told her that in spite of having to wear her old boarding school uniform, she still looked presentable. Her wide gray eyes were shadowed, however, proof of a restless night.

I wish I weren't always the new girl in school, she thought. But maybe today the others won't stare so much. It can't be as bad as yesterday.

"I'm leaving now!" she called out to her mother.

Mrs. Price hurried into the hall. "Is it really that late already?" She kissed Kathy's smooth cheek. "Have a good day," she said.

"You, too." Kathy picked up her books from the hall table and opened the door. "I'll be home at three."

As she left the large old house she had lived in less than a week, she saw her new friend, Marcie Clark, waiting at the end of the driveway. "Have you been here very long?"

"Exactly ten seconds," Marcie said. "We just had breakfast, and I like to take my time during meals. Gee, the painters sure did a great job on your house. I never thought the old McKenzie place would look this good again."

Kathy shifted her books from one arm to the other and looked back at the house she and her mother were occupying alone until her father joined them. "I like it better than any other place I've ever lived," she said. "But anything is better than a dormitory. We still haven't unpacked all the boxes yet, because Mom wants to wait until Dad gets here from Belgium and chooses one of the empty bedrooms for his study. And the boarding school still hasn't sent the rest of

1

my clothes. I wish I had something besides uniforms and weekend scruffies."

They walked briskly along the sidewalk, enjoying the clear, cool September morning. Port Borden, Washington, was comfortably sheltered in a small cove on Puget Sound. Late-summer roses bloomed in every yard, and the maple trees were showing a first hint of gold, while overhead a half dozen seagulls cried mournfully to each other. The rocky beach was only a few short blocks away, close enough for Kathy to smell the clean salt air. This really is a beautiful town, Kathy thought.

"I love this town," Marcie said, as though reading Kathy's mind. "But then, I've never lived anywhere else."

Kathy looked up at her and grinned. Marcie was half a head taller than Kathy, and looked rather sophisticated, with short, gleaming black hair. "You're lucky. We've moved so many times that I stopped counting. But this should be the last. I'm really tired of always being the new girl in school. It was nice of you to walk home with me yesterday. I was feeling like an orphan."

Marcie nodded. "I could tell. But as soon as you told me where you lived, I felt like celebrating. There hasn't been anyone my age living within a block of me since I was in kindergarten. How do you like the school?"

"It's a lot bigger than I thought it would be. I didn't know the students would come from the whole south half of the county." The size of the school had intimidated her on the first day. She was accustomed to small private schools, but in Port Borden there were more students in her English class than there had been in her entire sophomore class the year before. "I wish I didn't look so different from everyone else," she added ruefully. "But I've had to follow a dress code for the last few years." She looked down at her dark-green blazer and pleated gray wool skirt, then at Marcie's jeans and blue quilted down jacket. "I like what you're wearing better."

"My folks would love your clothes," Marcie said. "You look like a model. But I think you'd fit in better if you loosened up a bit. We're pretty casual here."

"I noticed that," Kathy said seriously. "I talked to Mom about it last night."

They were half a block from the school by then, and the sidewalk was crowded with noisy students, all heading toward the old brick building that was almost hidden by towering maples and poplars.

"It didn't cause a problem, did it?" Marcie asked. "My folks hate any discussion about clothes."

Kathy shook her head. "Oh, no. Mom understands. It's just that we're a little short of money right now, with the move and all. We didn't expect Dad's transfer so soon. I can't ask for new clothes for a while, and all I've got coming from my old school is either very dressy or too small."

Several girls called out greetings to Marcie and eyed Kathy cautiously. A few of them smiled, and Kathy was quick to smile back. She was experienced in making new friends, but still, her heart quickened and her palms were damp. It was never easy. She appreciated Marcie's cheerful companionship on her second day in the school.

Their lockers were in the same dark old hall, on opposite sides, and Kathy noticed that Marcie was surrounded by friends immediately while she put away her jacket and sorted through her books. Marcie saw her watching and beckoned to her. Kathy had been introduced to most of the girls the day before, and she had learned long ago to memorize names quickly. "Hi, Deb," she said to a blue-eyed girl who was no taller than she was, but whose blond hair was straight and worn shoulder-length.

"Hi, Kathy. It *is* Kathy, isn't it?" Deb Franklin's soft, little-girl face flushed with embarrassment.

"That's right," Kathy said. "Kathy Price."

Deb looked admiringly at her blazer and skirt. "Everyone's been talking about your clothes."

Kathy laughed. "You'll get bored quickly. Just about everything I own is a carbon copy of this."

A bell rang and the girls scattered in all directions. "See you at lunch," Deb called over her shoulder. Another girl, the one Kathy remembered as Liz Harper, was hurrying away beside Deb, and Kathy was suddenly chilled by the look Liz gave her.

"Sure, see you at lunch," she said to Deb. Auburn-haired Liz, who was one of the prettiest and best-dressed girls Kathy had ever seen, looked back once more at her, leaving Kathy to wonder what she had done to offend her. She watched until Deb and Liz were out of sight, then turned to Marcie. "I'll see you in English class."

Marcie was staring angrily down the hall. "I'll never know what Deb sees in Liz," she said crossly.

Kathy thought of the hostile look on Liz's face. "She doesn't seem very friendly."

"Ha!" Marcie said. "You don't know the half of it. See you later, Kathy." Marcie hurried away, and Kathy entered the nearest classroom door, where her French teacher was writing on the blackboard. The bell rang just as she slipped into her seat.

"You just made it, Your Highness." The boy sitting in the next seat smiled at her, blinking sleepily behind thick glasses.

"I'll do better tomorrow," Kathy whispered.

The teacher turned and began speaking rapidly to the class in French, but Kathy kept up easily. She looked at the boy who had spoken to her, pleased when he smiled at her again. He reminded her of a woolly bear cub. His thick brown hair curled low on his forehead, touching the frames of his heavy glasses. She guessed that he was not very tall, and his body was stocky and broad. He wore a heavy sweater, which accentuated his bearlike look. She returned his smile, then turned her attention to the front of the room. He had been friendly the day before, too, the only boy in any of her classes who had done anything more than stare. His smile was delightful, lighting up his brown eyes.

When the class was over, he asked her what class she had next, and he frowned when she told him she had English Lit on the third floor. "Too bad," he said. "I'm heading for the annex. But maybe we could meet at lunch. And by the way, I'm Andy Andrews, if you didn't happen to catch my name when the teacher was flaying me alive because of my accent."

"I'm Kathy Price, and I'm sorry, but I'm having lunch with Marcie Clark. Do you know her?"

"Everyone knows Marcie," he replied. "In this school, everyone knows everyone else."

"But it's so big," she said. She gathered her books together as she got out of her seat. "I'm not used to a school this large."

He studied the insignia on her blazer pocket. "I heard you were from a private school. A preppy," he said. "Did you start your junior year there?"

They walked to the door together, weaving between other students. Kathy kept her voice low. "Yes, my dad was transferred here unexpectedly, so Mom and I came here after I'd already started back to my old school."

Andy now looked like a worried bear. "No offense, gorgeous, but if I were you, I'd leave the rich-girl outfits at home."

Kathy stopped, shocked. "Listen," she said, "who said I was rich? I've been in boarding schools because my folks travel so much. I can't help it if my clothes are different."

"You're going to be late for class," Andy told her as he pulled her toward the stairs. "You don't have to explain anything to me, but the word's out that you're a snob."

Kathy walked beside him unwillingly, tears stinging her eyes. Suddenly she missed St. Catherine's, the boarding school she had stayed in for the last year while her parents lived in Belgium. She hadn't been there long enough to have formed the sort of friendships she had yearned for, but she seemed to have started out on the wrong foot at Port Borden High.

"Hey!" Andy said. "I didn't mean to shake you up. I was really only kidding you." He adjusted his glasses on his long nose and peered anxiously at her.

"Yes, I'll bet you were only kidding," Kathy said. "It didn't sound like a joke to me." She started up the stairs to the third floor, but when she looked over the banister, she saw him staring up at her with an expression of such dismay that she forgave him for his tactlessness.

Marcie was saving a seat for her on the aisle in the back, and when Kathy sat down, Marcie leaned toward her, whispering, "What's the matter? You look upset."

"I was talking to Andy Andrews, and he said something that bothered me a lot."

"Andy? He's a nice little guy, but sometimes his jokes aren't very funny."

"It was no joke," Kathy said. "He told me that some people think I'm a snob."

"It's that Liz!" Marcie hissed. "She's the biggest pain I've ever known. And the biggest gossip, too. She's just jealous, that's all." She glared at the next row, where Liz bent over her desk, her red hair hiding her face.

"You mean she's the one who's been saying those things about me?" Kathy whispered.

Just then the English teacher rapped on his desk with a pencil. "Kathleen? Marcie? Are your hearts really with us today?"

The class erupted with laughter as Kathy blushed.

"We'll talk about this later," Marcie whispered behind her hand.

"Marcie?" the teacher inquired politely. "May I interrupt your daily news report?"

"Sorry, Mr. Hawkins," Marcie said meekly as the class laughed again. Both girls concentrated on their notebooks, after exchanging embarrassed glances. Kathy was troubled. She'd talk to her mother again about the clothes problem. She had old jeans and a shirt or two that would do. Maybe if she removed the insignia from her blazers, they would pass as ordinary jackets. Her pencil flew over the page as she thought, but after a few minutes her mind wandered and she found herself looking out the window at the arch of blue sky streaked with clouds that looked thick as cream. Her father would arrive in a few days. The electronics company that employed him had arranged for the house and had had it painted and repaired, then moved her mother from Belgium and Kathy from Boston. For years she had adjusted to the loneliness of the changes, made new friends only to lose them again, and this was supposed to be their last move. Her father had been promoted to manager of the company's branch plant. No more consulting, he had said when her parents had told her about moving to Port Borden. They would have a real home at last.

She stared at the bright sky until her gray eyes burned. When the bell rang, she was so startled that she dropped her pencil in the aisle. As she reached down to pick it up, someone deliberately brushed against her shoulder, almost knocking her to the floor. She looked up to Liz's tight smile.

"Look out, Your Highness," Liz snapped. "You're so clumsy, you're dangerous."

She was gone then, leaving Kathy to fumble with her notes and books in silence.

"She's always like that," Marcie said. "Try to ignore her."

"What a great beginning," said Kathy as she laughed nervously. "There's nothing like making close friends right away."

"No girl can be friends with Liz unless she's rich or ugly," Marcie replied. "She likes to be surrounded by people who can show her off, my mom says."

Kathy and Marcie walked slowly out to the crowded hall. "But Deb isn't ugly, so I take it she's rich."

Marcie nodded. "And you're cute, but you live in the old McKenzie house. It's big, but it isn't a mansion, so even if you do wear private school clothes, Liz knows that you probably didn't get a new car for your sixteenth birthday."

"New car!" Kathy shouted with laughter. "I didn't get any kind of car! You mean Liz and Deb have their own cars?"

Marcie made a face. "Right. Isn't it enough to make you sick? Liz has a really expensive one, but Deb just has a little compact. I bet I'll be riding my old ten-speed bike until I'm thirty. Gee, my brother had to earn every cent he spent on that old wreck of his—I have to go to biology lab now," she interrupted herself, but then resumed what seemed to be a favorite subject. "Liz's mom drives a sports car with leather upholstery. If your mom looks anything like you, I can promise you that she's going to wait a long time before she's called to work with the library volunteers. Liz's mom heads that up and everything else in this town. You'll find out that Liz gets all her charm from her mother."

"Ugh," Kathy said. "I'll see you at lunch. We can talk more then."

"No, we can't, because Deb will be there. Like I told you, she seems to get along with Liz just fine. She's a real diplomat. Just take it easy though, and don't let Liz get you down."

Kathy walked to her next class alone, her mind busy with what Marcie had said. She knew one thing for certain. Marcie hated Liz, but Kathy was certain that Marcie had a good reason.

"Hey, prep school!" she heard. Her head jerked up and she looked around at the faces of the other students in the hall. Several of them were grinning at her, but not in a very friendly way. Bravely, she smiled back, but her eyes were checking out their clothes. She did stick out like a freak, she thought. Few of the girls wore skirts, and no one else had on what was so obviously a uniform. What was even worse, no one could possibly tell that she was not wearing the same blazer, skirt, and blouse she had worn the day before, because all of her uniforms were alike. She glanced down at the insignia again, vowing to remove it that very night.

History class was crowded and the room was overheated. The teacher droned on endlessly, boring Kathy into a stupor even while her eyes were drawn to the window again.

They'll forget all about my clothes in a few days, she told herself. Especially when I start dressing like them. I can fit in here. I can fit in anywhere. Goodness knows I've had enough practice.

She got little out of the lecture, and when the bell rang she bolted for the door along with the rest of the students. The cafeteria was at the other end of the building, but she wanted to stop at her locker first, to rid herself of the burden of books and papers, so she hurried blindly around a corner and ran into someone with enough force to knock her backward. She regained her balance with difficulty. Her books were scattered in all directions.

The boy she'd run into was a foot taller than she was, dark-haired and ruggedly handsome, with clear amber eyes that studied her thoughtfully. "Are you all right?" he asked. She saw that he was carrying a list of classes, and concluded that he must be new in the school, too.

"I'm all right," she said, light-headed and flustered. "Sorry. I nearly knocked you down, I guess."

"You'd have to be a lot bigger to do that much damage," he said. "Here, let me help you." He bent to pick up her books, and she knelt beside him.

"Well, well," a familiar and now hated voice exclaimed. Kathy looked up, to stare once more into Liz's cruel green eyes. Liz's friends watched eagerly. "I wonder if she'll turn back into a frog if we kiss her?" Liz asked. "And then will she disappear?"

Kathy's ears rang from the high-pitched shrieks of laughter. Liz tossed her head proudly, her red hair flickering about her shoulders like flames.

"I hope she doesn't disappear," the new boy said with lazy arrogance. "If she does, I'll find her and kiss her and change her back again." He smiled broadly at Kathy. "It would be my pleasure," he concluded.

Chapter 2

Kathy felt like a fool, crouched on the hall floor with Liz and her friends standing over her. She looked up courageously, meeting Liz's eyes, and was satisfied when she saw Liz's smile fade as she and her companions walked away. Kathy was glad that Deb wasn't among them. She didn't think Deb would be that mean.

"Who was that?" the new boy asked. He stood up, holding out Kathy's books, and she noticed then that he was wearing a beautiful, heavy silver ring on his right hand.

"Her name is Liz Harper," Kathy replied. "I don't think she likes me very much." She was going to ask him about his ring, just to change the subject, but he didn't give her a chance.

"Well, *I* like you," he said. "My name is Kevin Wade, and I see that you're new here, too." He handed her the class schedule she'd dropped.

"It's only my second day," she said.

"This is my first. In fact, I just got here an hour ago. Being late on your first day doesn't make you popular in the school attendance office, I found out, but I had a flat tire. What's your name?"

"Kathy Price," she told him. "I'm a junior."

"I'm a senior," Kevin said. "Hey, I'd better get going. See you around, Kathy. Okay?"

Kathy nodded and waved to him as he left. He's nice, she thought. And we have something in common. We're both new kids in school.

Marcie was waiting at Kathy's locker. "Where have you been? I'm starved, and they're serving macaroni and cheese for lunch. In this school, it's more macaroni than cheese, but I'm so hungry I'd eat the plate."

Kathy threw her books into her locker. "You're more broad-minded than I am," she said. "I hate macaroni and cheese."

"Then you and Deb can eat the cottage cheese salad," Marcie replied. "Although you don't need to go on a diet."

Kathy looked up. "Is Deb on a diet? What for?"

"Deb is always on a diet. I think she was born on a diet."

They walked into the cafeteria together and took their places in the line that snaked around the end of the counter and down the length of the large room. Several students said hello to Marcie; most stared at Kathy, but only a few spoke to her.

"I saw Liz again," Kathy said softly to Marcie.

"Oh, please!" Marcie cried, her black eyes snapping. "I don't want my appetite spoiled. If you mention her name, I won't even be able to swallow, and I'll bet we're even having yummy stale biscuits again."

Kathy looked behind the counter. "Actually, they don't seem too bad."

"You're looking at the napkins," said Marcie.

They inched forward toward the stack of trays. "Liz has second lunch, doesn't she?" Kathy said.

"Yes, and she was mad when Deb arranged her classes so that she could have first lunch. All of Liz's friends are supposed to have second lunch with her."

"Even if it interferes with the classes they really want?" Kathy reached for a tray, then chose silverware from the bins.

"Why should Liz care what anyone else wants when nearly everyone does exactly what she tells them to do?"

Kathy laughed a little nervously. "Hey, no one is that powerful!"

Marcie turned to look at Kathy, and the lopsided grin faded from her face. "You want to bet?" she said. "You just wait and see."

Marcie moved on, accepting a plate of macaroni and cheese from one of the perspiring cooks. Kathy lifted a salad from the tray of cracked ice and selected another plate with a slice of dark bread on it.

"If we kiss her, will she turn back into a frog?" Liz had asked. Remembering the sarcastic question hurt Kathy all over again, and when she and Marcie joined Deb at a table, Kathy was quiet and preoccupied. It wasn't a good beginning, she knew. The salad was hard to swallow, and not just because the cottage cheese was tasteless.

"A gorilla could cook better," Marcie grumbled as she ate.

"The cook *is* a gorilla," Deb said with a smirk. "Hey, I lost half a pound this week!" She finished her salad and attacked her chocolate pie enthusiastically.

"You just gained it back," Marcie told her. "Why don't you give up? You look great."

"Liz told me yesterday that I look like Andy Andrews," Deb said, eyes still on her pie, and Kathy and Marcie exchanged glances.

"I think he's nice," Kathy offered cautiously.

"Oh, Andy's a sweetie," Deb agreed. "But Liz hates him because he told everyone that she's tone deaf. In choir, he calls her Half Tone Harper and things like that." And to Kathy's relief, Deb burst out laughing. "Gee, she gets mad," Deb said. "Kathy, you should give up your study period and join choir. You'd love it. We have lots of fun."

Kathy hoped the relief she felt didn't show. It was going to be all right where Deb was concerned. She could count on her as a friend. "Maybe I will," she replied. "I always liked singing."

"Then we'll go to the office as soon as we finish, so you can check into choir this afternoon."

Marcie dropped her fork onto her plate. She hadn't finished her macaroni, but her milk carton was empty, and she had eaten Deb's biscuit as well as her own. "If I eat the rest of this goo, I'll probably die in trig," she said. "Are you two ready to go?"

"I sure am. That salad wasn't as bad as it looked," said Kathy. "But it was pretty bad." The other girls laughed delightedly.

"Tomorrow we have gorilla goulash," Deb announced. "I'm going to have two pieces of pie then. But let's go, you guys. The lunch break won't last forever, and if Kathy wants to switch to choir, we'd better get started."

The school secretary was out of the office when they got there, but the junior counselor filled out a new class schedule for Kathy. Afterward, Deb said good-bye to Marcie and Kathy in the hall and ran for her next class. Kathy and Marcie went in the opposite direction, but as they passed the student lounge Andy Andrews called out to them.

"Kathy just signed up for choir," Marcie told him.

"Oh, that's great," Andy said, bouncing around happily. "I hope you aren't a soprano. We've got so many now that I'm thinking of offering a bounty on them. Fifty cents a squeak."

"I'm an alto," Kathy offered.

"But are you any good?" Andy asked seriously, frowning at her through his dusty glasses.

Impulsively, Kathy answered, "I'm not bad. Actually, I'm pretty good." She felt suddenly confident and happier than she had been all day.

"Don't tell me I'm wrong, please," Andy cried. "Can it possibly be that you can sing on pitch?"

"Of course." Kathy laughed.

"Hey, world!" Andy shouted. "Kathy Price can sing on pitch!" He lowered his voice then, while the other students in the lounge watched, and whispered, "Liz Harper will have a fit. I can hardly wait. Old Half Tone Harper thinks she's the star alto, but she sings in the key of R."

Kathy smiled, but she suddenly felt as if she had eaten rocks for lunch.

Kathy's second day in trig class bewildered her just as much as her first day had. Miss Correy, the young and glamorous teacher, taught rapidly, moving along at a pace that left Kathy far behind. She seemed to be speaking another language, Kathy thought miserably. This had happened before, when she'd transferred from one school to another, and she resolved to ask her mother for help that night. Mrs. Price was good at math and she had rescued Kathy several times in grade school, during that wonderful time when the family had lived together for two whole years.

Kathy was depressed by the time the class was finally over. She hadn't understood anything the teacher had said, and the homework assignment would take hours. Marcie walked out the door with her, muttering crossly under her breath.

"Sorry," Kathy said. "I couldn't hear you."

"I said that Miss Correy was some sort of child prodigy when she was in school," Marcie repeated. "She thinks everyone is like her."

"Well, I'm not, that's for sure," replied Kathy.

"I got A's in algebra and geometry," Marcie grumbled. "But I'll be lucky to even pass this class."

"Maybe it'll get better."

"Maybe it'll get worse, you mean," said Marcie. "You've got botany now, right?"

"Yes, and I really love it, too," Kathy said. "I don't think I'll have any trouble there, at least. I'll see you after school at the lockers."

Marcie joined some other students walking toward the stairs, and Kathy went to the botany lab, which opened into a huge greenhouse. The whole area smelled of moist earth and geraniums. She could see them blooming in the back of the greenhouse, and she wrinkled her small nose appreciatively.

The class was crowded, and she had been in her seat for several minutes before she noticed that Kevin Wade, the boy with the silver ring, was sitting only three tables away from her. He was watching the teacher attentively, and Kathy thought that he probably hadn't seen her, but when the class went to the greenhouse, Kevin eased himself through the crowd of students until he was standing next to her.

"Hello again," he said.

She smiled up at him and would have spoken, but just then she saw Liz nearby, surrounded by several other girls. She hadn't noticed Liz in the class the day before, and she hoped Liz hadn't noticed her, either.

The teacher assigned tasks quickly and the students took their places. Kevin joined a group that was cutting back a long vine that was threatening to strangle some discouraged pineapple plants. Kathy was handed a package of bulbs and sent to the other end of the greenhouse. She saw Liz, armed with pruning shears, standing beside Kevin and tossing her flaming hair provocatively while she smiled at him. Noticing that Kevin seemed intrigued by Liz, Kathy bent down, looking away to hide her disappointment, and mechanically began planting bulbs.

Oh, well, she thought. Liz is pretty, and he's absolutely gorgeous. Why wouldn't they be attracted to each other?

The soil she worked in smelled good, and suddenly she became enthusiastic about her work. In spring, she would see the bulbs she'd planted bloom into beautiful daffodils. She decided to ask her mother if they could plant bulbs at home, to make the old house seem like it belonged to her family. In the spring, she would still be there, and every spring for years she could watch the bulbs she planted come up and bloom again.

"Hey, prep school!" someone hissed.

Kathy's daydream was shattered. She looked around quickly, but everyone near her was working busily. No one met her eyes.

"Hey, frog princess!"

She looked down then, determined not to show that she cared, and her little shovel smoothed the soil back in place over a bulb as if it were guided by someone else. I wish this day were over, she thought. At that moment, Port Borden didn't seem like such a nice place after all.

Chapter 3

The choir room was wild and noisy, and the teacher did nothing to encourage quiet for at least ten minutes. Students milled around, talking and laughing, while someone hammered out jazz on the piano, and in another corner of the big room a quartet attempted to rehearse without much success.

The teacher, a young man with curly brown hair and an even curlier beard, grinned while Andy introduced Kathy to him. "An alto, are you?" Mr. King asked. "Good. I can use you." He squinted at her through tinted glasses and his face puckered up impishly. "You're awfully little to be an alto. Want to sing a solo today?"

Kathy backed up, startled. "No!" she said. "I'd be too scared!"

Mr. King laughed at her. "There's nothing I like better than a scared alto. They try harder." He turned to the noisy students then, clapping his hands. "Class!" he shouted. "Settle down!"

The students went to their seats, and once again Kathy saw Kevin. This time he was deep in conversation with several boys.

"We have two new singers today!" Mr. King yelled over the chatter. The noise died down and curious eyes sought out Kathy and Kevin. Mr. King introduced them, and when he told the class Kathy's name, she heard a girl giggle. She blushed and hurried to the seat Mr. King assigned to her, between two girls in the last row. She put her books and purse on the floor under her chair, relaxed, and looked around the room.

Kevin had taken his place among the baritones, and Andy was sitting at the piano. When he saw Kathy looking at him, he winked comically.

Sheet music was passed out and Mr. King raised his baton. To Kathy's astonishment, the large, disorganized singing group was terrific. By the time the class was half-over, she had decided that it was the best school choir she had ever heard, and she was delighted to be a part of it. And Andy was not only a wonderful musician, he also had a remarkably clear tenor voice. He sang a brief solo with no apparent self-consciousness, and she envied him for that.

Then Mr. King pointed his baton at her. "Let's hear you now, Kathy," he said. "Take the second verse alone. It should be low enough for you."

All eyes were on her when she stood, so she was certain everyone could see the sheet music trembling in her hands. Andy gave her her pitch, and she began, but fright buzzed in her ears and she had no idea how she sounded. When she finished and sat down, she thought that the buzzing had grown louder until she was almost deaf from it. Andy was grinning at her, and Deb had turned around in her seat in the soprano section and was clapping excitedly.

They were all clapping, even Mr. King. All, that is, except for Liz and her friends. Liz was sitting several rows ahead; she turned around in her chair and stared at Kathy. You're in trouble, the look said clearly. You'd better watch out.

Mr. King rapped his baton on his music stand. "We have an alto soloist for the fall concert," he announced. "Welcome to the choir, Kathy Price. We've been looking for someone like you."

But Kathy's eyes were locked with Liz's, and at that moment she wished her family were moving again. Liz turned away, smirking, and she whispered something to the dark girl ahead of her. They both laughed and looked back at Kathy. She knew they hated her, but she didn't understand why.

* * *

Kathy didn't mention Liz on the way home. Sometimes, she decided, it's better not to tell anyone about your problem. It will go away sooner if you don't make too much of it.

When I can dress like the rest of them, and when they get used to seeing me, all this will be forgotten, she told herself firmly. At least she hoped so.

"Did you see that tall blond boy in trig?" Marcie was saying. "The one in the blue sweater?" She was eating again, this time a candy bar she had taken from her pocket.

Kathy shook her head. "No. What's his name?"

"Gordon Kelly," said Marcie, and she took another bite of the candy. "He wouldn't be very flattered if he knew you hadn't even noticed him. He sure noticed you."

"The only thing I remember about that class is how stupid I was," Kathy said unhappily. She scuffed her shoes along the sidewalk, kicking at scattered leaves that fell from the birch trees as they walked beneath them. "I'll be up all night with the homework."

"So will everyone else, except Gordon. He's a math genius, which brings me to the big question."

"What big question?"

Marcie's mischievous eyes sparkled. "He asked me if I thought you'd go out with him. I told him I didn't know, but you'd probably appreciate some help with trig and, for that matter, so would I." She laughed good-naturedly. "He didn't take the hint, I'm sorry to say. All he wanted to talk about was you. But if you don't even remember him..."

Kathy shrugged. "Gee, I'm sorry, but I really don't. And I can probably handle the math myself." With a lot of help from Mom, she added silently.

Marcie shifted her books to a more comfortable position. "You don't sound very enthusiastic about him. He's awfully cute. He was going with Liz until the end of summer, but they split up for some reason. She'd kill him if she knew he was interested in you. I think she's trying to get him back."

"I wish she were," Kathy said, thinking of the way Liz had smiled at Kevin during botany.

They had reached Kathy's house by then and were standing at the end of the driveway, under a maple tree that glowed brilliantly against the bright September day.

"Hey, there's someone under your car," Marcie said. "I see legs sticking out."

Kathy saw her mother's legs protruding from under the used car they had bought the week before. "That's just my mom."

"Your mom?" Marcie laughed. "What is she doing?"

"Trying to fix the car, I guess. It isn't working right, and she's good at that sort of thing."

Mrs. Price slid out from under the station wagon and wiped her face and hands on an old towel. "Kathy! Is it three o'clock already?"

"Come on and meet her," Kathy said to Marcie, and Marcie followed her up the driveway to where Mrs. Price was waiting.

"It's easy to see where Kathy got her looks," Marcie commented, as casually as if she were an old family friend. "When you're done with your car, would you have a peek at my bike? The brakes don't work very well and every time my dad touches it, he makes it worse."

"You bring it over and I'll try my best," Mrs. Price replied. She was wearing an old sweat shirt with "Chief Mechanic" printed on it and faded jeans, and didn't look much older than Kathy. "You've caught me at a disadvantage, Marcie," she said cheerfully. "As you can see, I'm wearing last year's designer outfit. But won't you come in for hot chocolate with us?"

"I never turn down food," said Marcie. "Do you really know what's wrong with your car?"

Mrs. Price led the way into the house. "Indeed I do. I took a course in auto mechanics a couple of years ago. My only problem is I don't have the right tools yet."

Kathy showed Marcie where to leave her books in the wide front hall. "I guess we bought a lemon, then," she said. "Maybe we should have waited for Dad."

"Don't give up on me yet," Mrs. Price replied. She invited Marcie into the kitchen and took another mug down from the cupboard. A pot of hot chocolate was steaming on the stove, and the white kitchen table had been set with blue placemats, a plate of butterscotch cookies, and two thick white mugs with blue flowers on them. Kathy got another blue napkin from the kitchen buffet, and Mrs. Price filled the mugs with foamy dark chocolate.

Marcie sat down, grinning. "Boy, is my mom going to love you," she said. "She's an awful cook and has to buy cookies from the bakery."

"She'd recognize these, then," said Mrs. Price as she passed the plate. "I just bought them at the bakery an hour ago."

Marcie helped herself to two cookies. "At home we have what my brother Tom calls 'survival desserts.' We're lucky if we survive. Mom's especially deadly where cake and cookies are concerned."

Mrs. Price smiled and said, "So was I, so I finally admitted it to myself and stopped trying. But I can do wonders with things from the freezer."

Marcie took another cookie. "Not my mom," she replied glumly. "Canned or frozen, it's all the same to her. She dumps food into a pot and heats it until it smokes and then calls us in for dinner. That's why I'm the only one in school who can eat the cafeteria food without needing medical care." She licked the crumbs off her lip carefully. "But Mom can sew better than anyone else. I've got lots of clothes, but I'm starving to death."

"Sure you are," Kathy said. "You've eaten enough today to keep the whole town alive for a month."

"Not yet, but I will have by the time I go to bed tonight," said Marcie. She stood up then and thanked Mrs. Price for the snack. She had hours of homework ahead of her, she explained, so she couldn't stay any longer.

Kathy walked with her to the front door and handed her her books. "I'll see you tomorrow morning."

"I'll be here," Marcie promised. Then she lowered her

voice. "I like your mom. She's nice. Different, but nice."
She clattered down the wide front steps and turned back to
wave. "Take it easy with the trig."

Kathy made a face and waved before she shut the door.
Behind her, Mrs. Price commented, "What an attractive
girl! I wish I were that tall."

"Who doesn't?" replied Kathy. "She's really nice, too.
Hey, do you have time to help me with trig tonight?"

"Sure," Mrs. Price said. She had started up the stairs to
the second floor, but she stopped then. "Is something wrong,
Kathy? You've looked upset ever since you got home."

Kathy shook her head. "No, nothing's wrong except my
fatal ignorance. Trig's a hard subject here."

Mrs. Price walked slowly back down the stairs, her forehead wrinkled with a frown. "I think there's something
more," she said quietly. "Do you want to talk about it?"

Kathy hesitated, not wanting to add to her mother's problems. If the car needed repairs, then her mom probably
wouldn't appreciate hearing a request for new clothes.

"Kathy?"

Kathy looked down at her feet. "I guess I didn't have
too great a time today," she murmured.

Kathy sat down on the bottom step. "I feel like such a
dumb little kid," she said. "I know I shouldn't let it bother
me, but it does." And she told her mother everything.

Mrs. Price sat down next to her daughter and said, "That's
absolutely rotten. It really is." She thought for a moment,
then went on. "I don't know how much help I can be to
you right away, but I think we can come up with something
more suitable than what you've been wearing. Maybe your
old jeans won't be so bad. And some of my things might
fit you. But Kathy," she added quietly, "believe it or not,
there's a Liz in everyone's life. How much are you going
to let yourself care about what she thinks? You don't like
her, anyway. Are you going to let Liz decide whether or
not you're happy here?"

Kathy shook her head. "I guess not," she replied. Her
mother reached over and hugged her.

"Good!" she said. "Now I'm going upstairs to take a shower. If you'll start the chicken, I'll make a salad when I get down."

Kathy went back to the kitchen and hung her green blazer over the back of a chair.

Am I going to let Liz decide whether or not I'm happy? she asked herself as she took the chicken out of the refrigerator.

I don't want to, but so far she seems to be doing just that.

Late-afternoon sun streamed in the window, warming the pleasant, fragrant old room, but Kathy, covered with a big apron and hurrying between stove and counter, never saw the golden glow surrounding her.

She was remembering Liz's green eyes, cold and hard as glass.

Chapter 4

The school cafeteria was noisier than usual, Kathy thought, but there was a good reason. The drama club clowns were performing in one corner of the room, trying out their talent show act, and they had a long way to go before their antics were polished and professional. The students applauded them, however, especially the short clown with the small red umbrella stuck through his black derby hat. Kathy suspected that the "Rainmaker," as he called himself, was Andy Andrews. The baggy costume and heavy makeup were a good disguise, but his animated gestures gave him away. After the clowns bowed and blew kisses on their way out the door, Kathy turned her attention back to her two friends.

Deb was having cottage cheese for lunch again, but two pieces of chocolate pie flanked her salad plate this time. "How's the goulash?" she asked Kathy.

Kathy made a face. "If I think about something else, it's not so bad."

"Hey, it's great today!" Marcie insisted. "You should have been here last week. I don't think it was dead yet." She scraped her fork across her plate eagerly, gathering up every morsel. "I'm going to have to go back for seconds." She eyed Deb's double helping of pie. "Do you want me to get you another piece of pie, beanpole?"

"The cook already said no," Deb said serenely, and everyone at their table laughed. She glanced at Kathy then, and grinned. "I love your jacket. You're looking good, Kathy."

23

Kathy glanced down at the tweed jacket she had borrowed from her mom. No need to tell them that it's not mine, she thought, feeling slightly dishonest. The jeans were hers, though, and the beige blouse had been a birthday present from her grandmother. But the gold chain around her neck belonged to her mom, too. Jewelry had not been allowed at St. Catherine's. She felt much more comfortable in these clothes, and so far no one had called her "Your Highness" or "prep school." But then, no one except Deb, Marcie, and Andy had talked to her, either.

Stop worrying, she told herself firmly. The day isn't over yet. And it can't possibly be worse than yesterday.

"Are you ready for trig?" she asked Marcie when the girl returned to their table with another plate of goulash.

Marcie rolled her eyes toward the ceiling. "You jest, of course," she groaned. "As a matter of fact, I did finish the assignment. It's just one thousand percent wrong, that's all."

"That's my fault." Deb looked stricken. "When Tom asked me to come over and play pool, I should have said no. Then you would have spent more time on your homework."

Marcie's brother Tom was a senior. He and Deb dated casually, Marcie had told Kathy, even though Liz didn't like it. Tom played on the school football team, and Kathy had noticed that he had all of his sister's good looks, translated into masculine ruggedness. Liz had wanted him for herself, Marcie had said, her eyes sparkling with mischief. But Tom liked Deb better.

Marcie slumped in her chair. "I couldn't resist showing off last night. I can beat Tom at pool anyday, but I'm going to pay for it next period."

Deb giggled as she attacked her first piece of pie. "Marcie is a real pool shark," she told Kathy. "Her dad taught her, so don't let her set you up."

"I'll remember that." Kathy didn't know how to play pool, but she wished she had been invited to Marcie's the night before. She had spent the evening working, first on her homework, and then going through her closet with her mother. Both activities had been depressing.

"Gordon came over to see Tom." Marcie looked at Kathy from the corner of her eye. "He talks about you a lot. Why don't you try smiling at him in trig? He'll probably pass out."

"Which one is he?"

"The tall blond one. He plays basketball, and his dad is the track coach here. I'll point him out to you, but you'll recognize him, anyway. He'll be the one staring at you."

Kathy nodded silently. Her heart beat a little faster, but she didn't want to tell her friends she was nervous. She had never had a real date, but no one would admit something like that, she thought. Oh, there had been a few dances at St. Catherine's, but the boys had been imported in a group from a nearby boys school, and they never bothered hiding their boredom. Once in a while one of them would invite a girl to a movie, but this happened so seldom that Kathy had never wasted energy wishing it would happen to her, and it never had.

Deb finished her second piece of pie and patted her flat stomach. "A diet is only bearable if you have dessert."

Marcie tapped her head with her forefinger. "Deb's crazy, you know," she said, and Kathy laughed.

They carried their trays to the counter in single file, and as Kathy waited for her friends to unload their dirty dishes, she became aware of several people passing close behind her. The back of her neck prickled even before she heard someone whisper, "Hey, prep school!" It was a girl's voice, but Kathy didn't recognize it. She refused to turn around and was grateful that Deb and Marcie had not seemed to hear.

This will stop sooner or later, she told herself. I can wait it out.

But she went to her next class quiet and sober-faced. The sky was clouding up outside, and the weather matched her mood.

As soon as Marcie took her seat in trig, she caught Kathy's eye and pointed to the back of a tall blond boy who was pulling sheets of paper out of a folder. As if on cue, the boy turned around and looked at Kathy.

She blinked. His face was tanned and his blond hair was streaked from the sun, so his bright-blue eyes seemed as brilliant as sapphires. He smiled, showing even white teeth, and Kathy was immediately reminded of the three years she had spent wearing braces. He wouldn't have spent even five minutes in an orthodontist's office. Probably he didn't have a single filling in those perfect teeth.

He looks like an actor, she decided. He even has a dimple in his chin.

Unaccountably she blushed, and she heard him laugh. When she looked over at Marcie, she saw her friend smiling.

So that's Gordon, Kathy thought, and she was impressed. No wonder Liz wants him back. I feel sorry for any girl who goes out with him. Liz will eat her for lunch.

She took out her homework and dismissed Gordon from her thoughts. He was probably friendly to everyone.

The teacher rattled along at a fast pace again, too fast for Kathy. By the time the bell rang, she was seriously considering dropping the class. For some reason, she couldn't understand most of what the teacher said. Even with her mother's help, she doubted that she could make it through the end of the semester. Not at the rate she was going.

She saw that Marcie wore a look of helplessness that must have matched her own. We're having the same problem, Kathy thought, but she wasn't comforted.

When she and Marcie left, they found Gordon waiting outside the classroom door. Kathy suspected that this had been prearranged, but she stopped with Marcie, hoping her smile hid her panic.

"Kathy, this is Gordon," Marcie said quickly. "I gotta go now. See you later, at the lockers."

She was gone before Kathy could protest. Gordon was studying her face, and she felt a blush rising on her cheeks again.

"That's cute, you know." His smile dazzled her.

"What is?"

"Your blush. You turn pink every time I look at you."

Kathy edged past him nervously. She felt like a twelve-year-old, stupid and awkward. "I'd better go," she said softly. "I don't want to be late. I'll see you later, Gordon. Okay?"

"You bet you will." He laughed as she rushed away, and Kathy hated herself. Why did I say I'd see him later? she raged at herself. It sounded as if I'm expecting him to meet me after school.

She was still fretting when she reached botany class, and the first person she saw was Liz, standing by Kevin's table, talking animatedly, her hair shining in the light from the window.

Liz ignored her as she walked past, but Kevin called out, "Hi, Kathy." She smiled back at him and nodded politely at Liz, but the redhead looked away, as though Kathy were invisible.

Kathy slid into her seat, pretending an indifference she didn't feel. Kevin was running one hand through his heavy dark hair, and she saw the silver ring gleaming on his finger. He's really nice, she thought. Too nice for Liz.

When class was over, Kevin appeared beside Kathy's chair, smiling in an easy, friendly way. "Can I walk you to choir?"

He was wearing a sweater that matched his amber eyes, intensifying their color. He has tiger eyes, Kathy thought, astonished. No, panther eyes. That black hair and those yellow eyes. Oh, he's much better-looking than Gordon, but not in that theatrical way. He looks like someone who would like being outdoors. Maybe . . .

"What?" she asked confusedly.

"I asked you if I could walk you to choir," he repeated, laughing.

She nodded happily. She knew Liz was watching them. Too bad, she thought. You can't have everything your way. She felt a surge of triumph and was glad that Kevin had singled her out. "Your ring is really beautiful," she said. "I noticed it yesterday."

Kevin looked down at his ring and smiled wistfully. "My grandfather gave it to me, just before he died. He made it when he was a young man." He held his hand out so that

Kathy could see the ring better. It was intricately carved
with a pattern of overlapping leaves. Kathy had never seen
anything like it.

"Your grandfather made it?"

"He was a silversmith. He taught my dad and Dad taught
me."

Kathy stared at him. "You mean you know how to make
silverware?"

Kevin laughed. "No, I can't do that, but Grandfather
could. My dad and I design silver jewelry as a hobby."

Kathy shook her head in amazement. "I don't even know
how jewelry is made. I never thought about it before. I
guess I must have thought that it grew on magic trees."

"Not quite," Kevin said. "But I like that idea." He smiled
down at her as if he thought she were special, and in that
delicious moment, she thought she was, too.

They could have found the choir room in the dark because
of the noise that spilled out into the hall. The rooms surrounding the choir room all had closed doors. Kathy grinned.
Being one of Mr. King's neighbors could not be easy.

This time she stacked her books on the long, shabby
table that leaned against one wall of the room. She had seen
the other students put their books there, and it was better
than the dusty floor where she had left her things the day
before.

Andy waved at her from the piano. He still had a streak
of clown makeup on his chin. "Hi, Rainmaker," she murmured as she passed him.

"Aww," he groaned. "Nobody was supposed to know."

"You told me everyone knows everyone else in this
school." She was pleased when she heard him say, "You
catch on fast, Your Highness." It didn't hurt anymore when
he teased her, because there was no malice in him. He wasn't
like Liz and her friends.

The class ended too quickly. She couldn't believe that
fifty minutes had passed until she looked at the clock. Mr.
King darted about, collecting music and laughing at his own
jokes, while the students lined up to retrieve their books
from the table; but when Kathy got to the table, she dis-

covered that her books and leather purse were gone.

She looked around bewilderedly. Kevin and Andy were behind her, talking to Deb. Most of the other students had already left the class.

"My books and purse are gone," she told Deb. "I left them right here, on this corner of the table."

All of them stared at the table, mystified. There were three stacks of books left, and Deb's purse topped one of them. "Are you sure?" Deb asked.

Kathy nodded miserably.

"It must be some sort of mistake," Deb said in a small voice. "Nobody in this class would steal."

Kathy ran her fingers through her curly hair distractedly. "My locker key was in my purse. I haven't even met my locker partner yet, so I don't know how I'm going to get my French book."

"I'll bet your locker partner is Pris Burke," Deb offered. "She's been out with the flu. But the custodian can open your locker. C'mon, let's catch him before he leaves for the day."

The girls waved a quick good-bye to Kevin and Andy and ran toward the custodian's office. The old man was irritated with Kathy, but he shuffled off to her locker, jingling an enormous key ring, and all the time he was trying keys in her lock he grumbled under his breath. At last the door swung open, and Kathy thanked him fervently.

"You girls," he complained. "You're always forgetting where you left your keys."

"But I didn't!" Kathy protested. "I already told you that someone took my purse!"

"Sure, that's what you say," he grumbled sourly. "Well, that's not my problem. Go tell 'em in the office."

He shuffled away then, with one last angry look at Kathy.

Deb watched him leave. "That old grouch! He's been here since the Flood and doesn't care what happens to anyone." She turned back to Kathy. "I'd better go get my stuff out of my own locker. Do you want me to go with you when you go to the office?"

"No, but thanks, anyway," Kathy said. "I'll just get my

French book and tell Marcie where I'm going. Darn it! My trig book and homework assignment are gone, too."

"They'll get you another book," Deb assured her before she ran off.

"Unfortunately," Kathy muttered under her breath as she reached up and took her French book off the shelf. A small sheet of paper fluttered down to the floor, so she bent to pick it up. On the paper, someone had drawn a crude sketch of an ugly frog with a crown on its head.

Kathy was still staring at the picture when Marcie joined her. Kathy handed her the sketch and explained what had happened.

"I bet Liz did this!" Marcie said angrily. "It's just the sort of thing that she would do. I wish we could prove she took your purse and left this in your locker. I'd love to see her kicked out of school." She slammed the locker door shut. "Come on, Kathy. Let's go to the office. And you can move in with Bibi and me until you get a new key. There's always room for one more."

Kathy was aware of a sharp pain behind her eyes. This is so darned mean, she thought. Why won't Liz leave me alone? What did I ever do to her?

Then she remembered. It was because of Kevin. Liz had wanted him for herself, and she was showing Kathy just how rough she could play when someone interfered with her plans.

Well, we'll just see about that, Kathy thought furiously. Maybe everyone else gives in to you, but I won't. You've got a big surprise in store for you, Liz Harper. I've had enough!

Chapter 5

Kathy was awake late that night, working on the math problems that Marcie had copied from her own book and given to her after school. "You'd better not skip an assignment," Marcie had told her. "Miss Correy's specialty is throwing big scenes in class." The tall girl's sober expression was convincing.

Now Kathy labored over the problems, even though her watch told her that midnight was drawing near. Her class notes had been stolen, too, making her task even more difficult. The usually tidy desk was littered with crumpled papers and she was close to angry tears. Outside her bedroom window, an enormous autumn moon hung placidly against a dark-blue velvet sky, and once she put down her pencil and looked out at it for a few minutes. The unusual beauty of the night did not escape her, but it did not console her, either. She pulled her quilted robe close and sighed unhappily. How could everything have gone so wrong?

She bit her lip to distract herself from the tears that were ready to spill down her cheeks, then bent her head over her homework again. When she finished it, the clock in the living room downstairs was striking the half hour. Twelve-thirty, she thought, and I'm still not sure I've got the right answers, but I'm tired of trying.

Later, lying in bed, she thought of Liz again and resolved to stand strong against anything and everything that the girl could come up with to torment her. I'll outlast her, Kathy told herself. No matter what, I'll simply keep going.

But when she finally slept, she dreamed restlessly of St. Catherine's, where her days had been well ordered and her teachers eager to help. And there had been no Liz among the friendly girls.

The next two days passed slowly. Her stolen books were replaced with expensive new ones, and Kathy never let them out of her sight unless they were stored in her locker. She kept her new locker key in the pocket of her jeans.

On Friday, her locker partner returned to school after a long bout with the flu, and Kathy met Pris Burke for the first time. Pris was painfully thin, with sloping shoulders that hunched protectively over the books she held close to her flat chest. Her complexion was poor, her brown hair dry, and her small watery eyes seemed to be irritated. She acknowledged Marcie's introduction by staring suspiciously at Kathy and then saying, "The top shelf is supposed to be mine!" Her voice was loud and shrill, attracting the attention of everyone in the hall.

Kathy apologized quickly and took her books from the shelf. "There was nothing on the shelf, so I thought it would be all right."

"That shelf has always been mine!" Pris complained. "And the hook on the right side is mine, too."

"Oh, for heaven's sake!" Marcie cried. "You always make such a fuss about everything! Kathy didn't hurt your shelf or your hook."

"But they're mine!" Pris whined, and she pulled Kathy's jacket out of the locker and thrust it at her.

"I said I'm sorry!" Kathy told her, but Pris walked away then, her head jerking angrily, and she didn't look back.

Marcie's laugh had a sharp edge. "That's Pris for you. She hasn't changed since first grade, and you can see why she usually has a locker to herself. No one can stand her."

"Maybe she still doesn't feel very well."

"Pris never feels very well," Marcie said. "She gets more colds than the whole junior class put together. And she's always falling over things or bumping into desks and then bawling about it. Then she puts bandages on her bandages."

"I think that's sad," said Kathy.

"You'll be making a mistake if you feel sorry for her," Marcie warned. "She's a troublemaker. What she doesn't know about people, she makes up, so Andy calls her the Daily Gazette. And if you try to be nice to her, she'll twist it around until you look like a monster. Believe me, I know from experience what Pris is like."

Kathy sighed disgustedly. "That's all I need right now."

"Why don't you just move in with Bibi and me permanently?" Marcie asked. "Bibi's great. She makes cookies in home ec and leaves them in the locker for me."

Kathy hung the tweed jacket on the left hook. "No, I'd crowd you too much. I'll try not to offend Pris any more than I already have, and I'll leave my books on the bottom of the locker. That ought to satisfy her." She slammed the locker door emphatically and tucked her cotton shirt securely inside her leather belt.

"Lots of luck with that idea," Marcie said with a grin. "Just don't let your stuff get in the way of Pris's broomstick. She won't have a way of getting home then."

Later, Kathy saw Pris talking to Liz, and Pris's blotchy face was flushed with nervous excitement. Kathy nodded politely as she passed, but both girls ignored her. So be it, she told herself. I can live without you, but you're not going to turn me into a rude clod.

The trig class was her hour of torment every day, and on Friday Miss Correy asked her to stay in the room after the bell rang. The two minutes Kathy spent at the teacher's desk were the most embarrassing yet. Her homework was barely acceptable, she was told, but her classwork definitely was not. "Boredom," she was told crisply, "is no excuse for shabby work." Kathy knew explanations would be useless. She promised she would try harder and then quickly left the room.

Marcie was waiting in the hall for her. "Did you get pep talk number ninety-seven?"

"No, I think I got ancient druid curse number one hundred

and one," Kathy replied, chagrined. "The more nervous I get, the worse I do."

Marcie pointed to Gordon, who was almost out of sight at the end of the long hall. "Gordon could help you." She grinned. "He'd love it."

"If Mom can't, nobody can," Kathy said grimly. "I wouldn't want him to know how stupid I am."

She had deliberately been avoiding Gordon. Every time he looked at her, she smiled politely and then looked away. There was something about him, a sophistication, perhaps, that caused her to be cautious. The poise that Marcie seemed to find so attractive in him overwhelmed Kathy, and sometimes she thought that he could read her mind, for his brilliant blue eyes seemed to examine her face knowingly. She found herself thinking about him at odd times and wondering what a date with him would be like. The thought made her uncomfortable.

But Andy was another sort entirely. She would never take him seriously, she knew, but his quick wit and infectious laughter delighted her, and she looked forward to the few minutes before choir each day when he singled her out for a chat. He had even suggested that she stay after school with him two afternoons a week to rehearse a duet. When they knew the music well enough, he said, they could audition for Mr. King and with any luck at all, be a part of the talent show in November. "And afterward," he had said happily, "I'll take you to the Beaux Arts Ball."

"Is it fun?" she asked.

"Oh, it's just great!" he cried, bouncing about and waving his arms. "Everyone from the music and art departments gets together and puts on this big formal dance. We sell tickets to the rest of the students to pay the expenses. You'll love it!"

Kathy grinned at him helplessly. He was irresistible. "I think I'd like that. Thanks."

Andy's face fell then, in mock dismay. "The only problem is that I play in the band, so I can't dance with you. But look at it as a blessing. I don't know how to dance!"

She couldn't help but laugh with him. "I'll manage," she promised him.

He winked solemnly. "Oh, I'll bet you will, Your Highness," he assured her.

Kevin had fallen into the habit of walking her from botany to choir every day, and secretly she was thrilled. He talked casually about both classes, but he never asked a personal question and he never volunteered any information about himself after the day he had explained about his silver ring and his hobby. After school, she had seen him driving away alone in his car, heading toward the Port Borden business district, and it occurred to her that he might have a job in the afternoons. When she mentioned this to Marcie on the way home, Marcie nodded.

"He told my brother that he works in his dad's pharmacy after school and on Saturdays." Marcie swallowed the taffy she had been chewing. "His dad bought the drugstore, and the whole family works there."

Kathy remembered then what her mother had told her about the drugstore. It was open until nine every night. Her favorite daydream, where Kevin asked her out, faded and died.

Why would he want a date with me, anyway? she thought. He's never even hinted at it. He treats me the way Andy does; I'm just his friend. If he ever took anyone out, it would be Liz.

"You want to stop by my house for hot chocolate?" she asked Marcie in an effort to distract herself.

"Naturally! Your mom makes an extra gallon now, since I've practically moved in," Marcie said.

They quickened their steps. A chill wind swirled dry leaves about their feet and more leaves flickered and tore away from the trees overhead. The air smelled damp and salty, and gray clouds hung low over the town. No moon would light the sky that night. Just as they turned in the Price driveway, rain began to splatter the sidewalk.

Kathy's mother was sitting in her car with a big smile

on her face. The engine was purring along steadily. "I fixed it!" she called to them triumphantly. "I really did it!"

She jumped out of the car and hugged both girls enthusiastically. "And I got a phone call from your dad," she told Kathy. "From New York! Oh, Kathy, he'll be home tonight!"

"This calls for a double celebration," Marcie said. "Let's eat!" She dug through her book bag and produced a crumpled paper sack. "Surprise! My mom sent along some horrid little concrete cookies for us. Shall I call an ambulance now or later?"

It was ten o'clock before Mr. Price arrived. Kathy heard the taxi first and she ran to the door, shouting, "Dad's here!" In a moment, she was down the steps with her arms outstretched, and her father picked her up as if she were still a small child and swung her around. Mrs. Price was close behind her daughter, and Kathy moved aside so that her parents could greet each other warmly. "There's nothing like coming home to two beautiful blondes," her dad said, laughing, and they helped him carry his luggage inside, out of the cold rain that had been falling all evening.

Mr. Price was a tall man whose hair had turned silver prematurely, and Kathy had always thought him handsome. But now he appeared weary as he looked around with a smile and complimented them on the work they had done decorating the old house.

Mrs. Price helped him off with his coat, but he would not let go of the large sack he carried. Kathy saw her parents exchange glances, and then her dad held out the sack to her. "Your mom asked me to do some shopping for you in New York. I hope I got all the sizes right."

While Mrs. Price brought her husband a cup of coffee, Kathy sat down on the floor and began pulling smaller packages out of the big sack. The labels on some of the garments inside took Kathy's breath away. She held up a beautiful navy-blue jacket and rubbed the soft fabric against her cheek. "Oh, Dad, I think you went overboard. I didn't need anything this expensive."

Her parents looked at each other with pleased expressions. "Your mom and I talked about it and we decided that you've been so patient all these years, never complaining about all the moves or the strange schools. That sort of behavior deserves a reward. I hope everything fits and it's what you would have chosen yourself."

Kathy looked up from the silky pale-blue shirt she had been holding. "I would never have dared to pick these things, but I'm sure glad you did. Gee, four shirts and a sweater, and the jacket is the most fantastic one I ever saw. Better even than Mom's." She dug down to the bottom of the sack and pulled out another package. "Jeans?" she asked. Her dad only grinned. She ripped back the paper. "Two pairs!"

She let her gifts fall to the carpet and got up to kiss her father. "You didn't need to do this, honestly," she said. "Your coming home was enough."

"I'm home to stay this time, Kathy," he replied, and she thought that she heard a catch in his voice. "We'll be a real family now." He stood and picked up his coat. "There's one more package," he said. "Your mom told me on the phone that your purse was stolen at school. I hope this makes up for it."

She took the last package and unwrapped it. A new leather purse, slim and black, gleamed in its elegant box. Inside Kathy found a new wallet and a small leather-covered address book. She looked up at him, her eyes glistening with tears.

"We wanted to take some of the hurt out of your experiences," her mother explained. "You've had such a hard time, and you've handled it better than most people could."

They sat together, the three of them, until the old clock struck midnight. It had been a wonderful evening, and when Kathy finally went to bed she felt more secure than she ever had before. They were a real family now, and whatever happened to them from that night on, they would meet it with the knowledge that they had each other for strength and comfort. If Liz sulked and schemed in Kathy's dreams that night, Kathy did not remember in the morning.

Chapter 6

Kathy spent two afternoons during the following week with Andy, rehearsing a duet in the choir room. They found that their voices blended well, and they learned the music without much effort. But Andy was a hard taskmaster, and he insisted that they continue rehearsing twice a week until the day of the auditions, even though everyone who heard them was convinced that they would be given a place in the talent show.

Mr. King, the choir instructor, also assigned Kathy a solo, which he wanted performed at the fall music festival, when the choir, the orchestra, and the jazz band would put on a performance to which everyone in Port Borden was invited. The music festival was set for a Friday evening in November, the night before the talent show and the Beaux Arts Ball, and Kathy was excited and anxious about both nights. Andy, experienced in performing in front of an audience, assured her that she had nothing to worry about, but she fretted until he threatened her with daily rehearsals.

One day, while she and Kevin worked side by side in the botany greenhouse, he said, "You have a nice voice. Did you ever think about singing professionally when you're out of school?"

Kathy shook her head and laughed. Her fingers kept busy pulling dead leaves off the geraniums, but her thoughts were in a jumble. His compliment meant more to her than any other she had been given. "No," she told him. "I've never wanted to do that."

"What would you like to do, then?"

She sat back on her heels, suddenly struck with a new and exciting thought. "I love this class." She looked around at the masses of flowers and rich foliage. "I could be a botanist, or a botany teacher. Or I could work in a flower shop."

Kevin grinned. "Or you could be a farmer. Or a forester."

She nodded eagerly, pleased at his interest. "What sort of plans do you have?"

He pulled loose a leaf that clung to his sweater and held it in his hand, looking at it thoughtfully. "Next year I start college. I'll study architecture, but I'll always like working with silver." He glanced at her quickly, then examined the leaf again. "I'll make silver leaves while you take care of real ones." He went back to work and then said abruptly, "You like Andy, don't you?"

"Oh, yes!" Kathy said enthusiastically. "He's such a nice guy, and so talented."

Kevin nodded. "Yes. He's a nice guy. I like him, too."

The teacher clapped his hands then, and the students crowded around the utility sinks to clean up. Kevin moved away from Kathy, joining another boy, but after class he waited outside the door for her and once again walked her to choir. They talked only about botany class then.

On the second afternoon she stayed after school to rehearse with Andy, Deb offered her a ride home because a wild storm was blowing across Puget Sound, drenching Port Borden. Deb, who had stayed behind for a conference with one of her teachers, met Kathy in the hall, and together they ran for the parking lot where Deb's compact car was parked.

"Do you want to stop off at the Sugar Shack for a soda?" Deb asked as she turned her key in the ignition.

Kathy looked at her watch. "I've got time before dinner," she said. "But I'm too cold for a soda."

"They serve hot chocolate with whipped cream. It's on my diet."

"Your diet!" Kathy scoffed. "Everything good is on your diet."

"Sure," Deb agreed happily. "What's the point of a diet if you can't enjoy it?"

Kathy laughed. "I don't know why you think you have to diet. You can't wear more than a size ten."

Deb frowned as she turned into the parking lot of the Sugar Shack. "It keeps the peace."

"What do you mean?"

Deb shrugged her shoulders. "As long as I tell Liz I'm on a diet, she lets up with the nasty remarks about my figure."

Kathy bit back a reply. It wouldn't do any good at all to remind Deb that Liz's opinion was probably based on jealousy, or worse. Kathy sometimes thought that Liz laid down rules for her friends to follow just because she needed to control people, and it didn't matter how stupid the rules were. But Deb seemed to be a bit of a rebel, and once again Kathy wondered why Liz and Deb, two such different girls, were friends. It was none of her business, of course, but it seemed to her that Deb needed Liz like she needed warts.

They found a table near the back of the little ice cream shop and both of them ordered hot chocolate, although Deb asked for a double portion of whipped cream.

"You and Andy sound good together," Deb said when their chocolate had been served. "And his band is just great, too. He wants to be a professional musician someday. And did he tell you that he's also going to be a part of the drama club's clown act at intermission during the music festival?"

Kathy sipped her chocolate. "Yes. He's going to have to be a quick-change artist that night. I wish I had half of his talent."

"He'll be famous someday, and we'll all be bragging that we knew him in high school." The whipped cream had left Deb with a white mustache and she licked her lips. "Is it true that you're going to the Beaux Arts Ball with him the next night, after the talent show?"

"Yes, but he told me that his band will be playing for the dance, so I'll really be on my own."

"Gordon will probably go without a date," Deb said thoughtfully. "Some of the guys do. He and Liz used to go steady, but they don't now, and she's already made plans to go to the ball with someone else. Gordon thinks you're cute. He tells everyone except Liz that." Deb laughed and finished her hot chocolate. "He wouldn't dare tell her."

Kathy shrugged. "I don't know anything about Gordon's plans. I hardly know him."

"Well, that's not his fault."

The shop door opened then, letting in a blast of cold, damp air, and both girls looked up. Liz and Pris Burke entered, and Liz's green eyes glittered as she walked to their table.

"I saw your car in the lot," she said to Deb. "I wondered how you had time to stop here when you didn't have time to go shopping with me after school."

"I stayed to talk to one of my teachers," Deb replied with an indifferent shrug.

Liz leveled a hard look at Kathy, but she spoke only to Deb. "I'll call you tonight," she said, and then she and Pris walked out. Pris had a triumphant look on her thin white face, and Kathy thought she was taking malicious pleasure in Liz's tantrum.

"Sorry if I got you in trouble," she said to Deb.

Deb was looking at the door through which Liz and Pris had just passed. "You didn't get me into trouble. Liz likes to boss people around. I've been ignoring her since grade school. When she gets like that, it's best just to pretend you don't care and hope she gets over it by the next day."

"You should be an ambassador." Kathy laughed. "You've got more tact than anyone I ever knew."

"It's not tact," Deb said with a grin. "I'm a coward."

But Kathy didn't think that Deb was a coward. Riding home with her, she considered the various possibilities and finally decided that Deb was able to stay detached from situations. She was completely different from Marcie, whose emotions changed from moment to moment, swinging through laughter to anger and back again, always exuberantly.

Kathy, however, was neither detached nor uninhibited. Her anger burned inside her sometimes, until her head throbbed and her stomach ached. She wished that she could be like either Deb or Marcie, for both of them had found ways of handling their feelings toward Liz, even though the ways were exactly opposite. And either one of them would probably handle the cruel teasing at school better than she was. Even though she was a familiar figure in the halls now, and her clothes were no different from the other girls', she still heard the hated "prep school" and "frog princess" every day. Perhaps she was not teased as often, but she was still hurt and angered by a hostility that she could not understand.

Deb let her off in front of her house, and Kathy ran to the porch to escape the driving rain. As soon as she opened the door, she could smell the pot roast her mother had promised Kathy and her dad for dinner.

"I'm home!" she called to her mother as she dumped her books on the hall table.

"You had a telephone call," Mrs. Price said as she came into the hall. "I wrote down the name and number, but he said he'd call back."

Kevin, Kathy thought. No, he wouldn't call her. Maybe he did walk her to choir every day, but he had never asked for her phone number.

"It's some boy named Gordon Kelly," Mrs. Price continued. "And Marcie called you, too. She says it's a life and death emergency." Mrs. Price laughed and went back to the kitchen.

Life and death emergency, Kathy thought, amused. To Marcie, running out of potato chips was a life and death emergency.

She looked at the note pad that sat on the table next to the telephone and considered Gordon's name thoughtfully before she tore off the sheet and shoved it in her pocket. She wouldn't call him back, she decided, but her heart skipped a beat. She dialed Marcie's number instead. "So what's the life and death emergency?" she asked her friend. "Did you run out of snacks?"

"You're mean!" Marcie complained. "I nearly starved to death today. There wasn't enough on my lunch plate to keep a mouse alive. I'd been slaving over the plans for decorating the civic center for the Beaux Arts Ball, so I got home just before I collapsed, although all Mom had around here were some horrible doughnuts she made this morning. Honestly, they clank if you drop them on a plate." Kathy could hear Marcie's mother laughing good-naturedly in the background.

"Oh, you poor thing," Kathy said. "Now tell me what the big emergency is."

"Gordon came by after school, supposedly to talk to Tom, but actually he wanted to talk to me. About you! Kathy, this guy is really getting serious about you. He wanted to know if I thought you'd go to a movie with him tomorrow night, and I told him to call you up and ask. Did he?"

Kathy felt in her pocket for the message her mother had written. "Yes, he did, but I wasn't home. I haven't called him back, and I'm not going to. I wouldn't know what to say."

"All you have to say is 'Why did you call?'" Marcie said. "Gordon will take it from there. He had a really great idea. Tomorrow Tom and Deb are going to the movies, and I'm going, too, because Jim Abbott invited me. He's a friend of Tom's, and I've known him since I was two years old. He's so boring that even his own mother falls asleep when he's talking, but a date's a date. Gordon said he was going to invite you, and then we could all ride together. Afterward, we'll go someplace to eat. Now don't refuse until you think it over, and then call him and say you're going, or I won't save you one of Mom's great doughnuts to hold your door open when summer comes."

Kathy considered Marcie's enthusiastic torrent of words, and the scrap of paper in her hand suddenly held the promise of an evening of fun with friends rather than an invitation into unknown territory.

"Hello? Are you still there or did you faint?" Marcie cried.

"I'm still here, and I'm thinking."

"Oh. That's what that strange noise was! Well, hurry up and make up your mind. My dinner's almost ready, and the dog has already left for the neighbors'. He's afraid he's going to be fed the leftovers tonight."

Kathy laughed helplessly. "You're really a nut, Marcie. All right, I'll go."

"Yea! Great! You won't be sorry, honestly. Just think of me, with old Jolly Jim, and you'll know how lucky you are. For that matter, think about poor Deb, stuck with my dumb brother. Hey, I gotta go. I'll talk to you later." And Marcie hung up quickly, leaving Kathy to suspect that dinner had just been announced. It was wonderful, having such a funny, enthusiastic friend, and Kathy smiled all through dinner. A first date wouldn't be too bad, not if her two best friends were along, she thought comfortably.

Her parents accepted the news more calmly than she had expected. Her father only said, "I hope we get to meet this Gordon before you go out with him."

"Of course, Dad!" Kathy exclaimed. "I'm certain he plans on picking me up here." No other arrangement had even occurred to her, although she had not yet returned Gordon's call. Suddenly the pie her mother had brought home from the bakery did not seem to taste as good as it had before, and she put down her fork. Perhaps she should have called Gordon before speaking to her parents, but she had hoped he would call her back.

Maybe he'd changed his mind.

"Well, it's not definite yet," Kathy said quietly. "Marcie and I were just talking about it, that's all."

Her parents exchanged glances, as though they were reading each other's minds, but neither of them said a word.

She helped her mother clear the table in silence, and then she went to her room, with the excuse that she had homework to do. When the phone rang, it seemed to her that her heart stopped, and she pressed her hand to her mouth. She did not know whether she wanted the caller to be Gordon or not. The more time that passed, the less certain she was.

Her mother called her to the phone and settled Kathy's apprehension by telling her that Gordon was on the line. Why couldn't it be Kevin? Kathy thought. But it wasn't and it probably never would be.

Cheerfully, Gordon asked her to the movie, as if it had never crossed his mind that she might refuse. Kathy didn't tell him that she and Marcie had already discussed the evening, but instead she simply accepted his invitation, saying, "I'd like that. Thanks for asking me."

"I'll come by your house about seven tomorrow." He thanked her and hung up before she had a chance to change her mind.

And change her mind was exactly what she wanted to do. There was something about Gordon that made her uneasy, an undefinable quality that made her want to stay a little girl and not venture out into the adult world of dating.

But, she thought unhappily, I wouldn't have felt that way if it had been Kevin who'd called. The tall, dark boy, with his crooked grin, was nearly always on her mind. It distressed her to consider how much of her life revolved around the brief walks between botany and choir. It was as if each day led up to that few minutes, and when the walk was over, the day was over, too.

Chapter 7

During lunch on Friday, Marcie and Deb told Kathy that it had been decided that the three couples would meet outside the theater at eight o'clock that evening, and after the movie ended they would ride in Jim's car to a small restaurant. Later they would return to their own cars, Deb said. Kathy hid her dismay. That plan would leave her alone with Gordon twice in the evening, and she hadn't counted on that. Her inexperience worried her. He would, of course, think she was the biggest bore he had ever met. She knew she would not be able to think of anything to say to him when they were alone, and she was too ashamed to ask Marcie and Deb for hints, since neither of them knew that this would be her first date.

Gordon caught up with her in the hall, when she was walking with Kevin to the choir room, and he told her that he would pick her up at seven-thirty rather than seven. He grinned at Kevin and slapped him on the shoulder. "Take care of my girl," he said before he ran back down the hall.

There had not been time for Kathy to say anything. Her face burned and she could not meet Kevin's eyes. Why had that happened when she was walking with Kevin? It couldn't have been a worse time. It was almost as if Gordon had done it deliberately. Surely he could have told her about the change in his plans before or after trig.

But then, perhaps he hadn't known himself. Inwardly, Kathy sighed.

"I thought you were going with Andy," Kevin said. He looked straight ahead, and Kathy's heart sank.

"No, of course not!" she replied. "Andy and I are just friends. We're in choir together, and we're going to try out for the talent show."

"And you're going to the dance with him afterward," Kevin said quietly.

How had he found that out? Sometimes it seemed to her that all the students at Port Borden High did was gossip about each other. "We're just friends," she insisted.

Kevin looked down at her sheepishly. "I'm sorry, Kathy. You don't owe me any explanations about anything."

But she wanted desperately to explain. "And I'm only going to a movie with Gordon. Two of my friends are going, too."

"Hey, Kathy, I said you don't have to explain," Kevin reminded her. "I don't take attendance records. I leave that up to the school."

But all through the botany lecture she watched him, and she never heard a word the teacher said. Kevin has the wrong idea, she thought. If only I could have explained it better.

But then, maybe he isn't interested. He told me that I didn't have to explain.

The class was nearly over when the teacher asked Liz to pass out some information sheets. When the smartly dressed girl passed Kathy's table, she bent down and whispered, "My mom had a shirt like that, but we put it in the charity barrel at church. I'm *so* glad you're the one who got it."

"Oh, shut up!" Kathy said aloud, angrily, and when the students around her began to laugh, she blushed. Liz walked away with a self-satisfied smirk, and Kathy raged inwardly. Kevin gave no indication of having heard, but she was certain that Liz would tell him that she had succeeded in humiliating the frog princess again.

Well, I just won't let myself care, she told herself sternly. I've got better things to do with my time than feel miserable about Liz!

* * *

As soon as she got home from school she washed her
hair, and while it dried she pressed her best skirt and the
beautiful pink lambs-wool sweater that her father had brought
her from New York. Marcie called her twice, once to find
out what she was wearing, and once to tell her that she had
discovered a blemish on her chin and was thinking of killing
herself.

"You're only going out with Jim, remember? He's the
one who bores his own mother," Kathy reminded her.

"Yes, but you're going out with gorgeous Gordon, and
I know you don't care about him one way or the other,"
Marcie explained. "I had hoped I'd impress him enough so
that when you got tired of him, he'd think of me as someone
besides Tom's sister who beats everyone at pool."

Kathy inspected her fingernails while she talked. "Listen,
if you want, we can trade dates right now. The more I think
of it, the more I'm sure I belong with Jim. Bores ought to
keep each other company."

Marcie hooted with laughter. "Wait until you meet him.
All he talks about is his dad's new car or how many points
he made last basketball season." When she hung up, Kathy
was cheerful again, but the mood didn't last. She was uneasy; it was almost as if she could predict that the evening
was not going to go well.

That's silly, she told herself. But the feeling would not
go away.

She was ready by a quarter after seven, and she sat in
the living room with her parents, who were watching television. She did not want them to sense her apprehension,
so she pretended to look at a magazine. The clock's ticking
seemed to have slowed down. Kathy found herself com-
paring the old clock with her watch over and over, but when
the half-hour chime sounded, she was startled and the magazine slipped from her lap. Both her parents looked at her.

"I'd better get my coat," she said.

"It's about that time," her father said calmly.

Kathy took her coat out of the hall closet, and when she

returned to the living room she sat with the coat across her lap. It seemed to her that the volume on the television set had suddenly turned up without anyone touching it. The commercials blared and screeched, but her parents did not seem to notice. Even the ticking of the clock seemed louder. Kathy found herself watching it with fascination as the minutes ticked by.

At a quarter to eight, Kathy cleared her throat. "It looks like Gordon is going to be late."

Her mother glanced sympathetically at her, but Kathy's father was frowning.

"Maybe he had car trouble," Mrs. Price offered.

"Maybe," Kathy's dad said. He did not sound convinced.

At eight o'clock, Kathy went upstairs and locked herself in her bathroom. She ran cold water in the basin until her fingers were numb, then she splashed her face. All the time the water ran, she thought that she heard the doorbell ringing, but when she turned the faucet off, she knew the sound had only been in her imagination. She lingered upstairs for ten minutes, and then returned to the living room.

"I think I've been stood up," she said quietly. She was humiliated in front of her parents and close to tears.

At that moment the phone rang, and she hurried to answer it, praying that it was Gordon and that he had an excuse that would be sufficient to wipe the dark scowl from her father's face.

But it was Marcie instead. "Where on earth are you two?" she demanded. "The film starts in five minutes!"

"I guess you'd better go on in," Kathy told her. "Gordon seems to have been delayed."

"Wait a minute," Marcie said. Kathy could hear her talking to someone, probably Tom, and her friend sounded furious. When she came back on the line, her voice was trembling with anger. "Tom says he'll come and pick you up, so you won't miss much of the movie. He'll be there in just a few minutes."

"No!" Kathy blurted. "I don't want him to do that. He'll miss the beginning of the film, and anyway, I don't really want to go. You have a good time. It's okay."

"No, it most certainly isn't okay!" Marcie insisted. "I don't know what's going on, but Tom says that Gordon isn't always on time. But it's been, let's see, it's been forty-five minutes since he was supposed to pick you up. I think this is rotten. Let Tom come and get you! He won't mind. He's pretty mad, too."

"No," Kathy said. "I'm going to hang up now, Marcie, and I really mean it. I'm not going. We'll talk about this some other time."

Before Marcie could protest, Kathy hung up the phone. Her parents were staring at her, waiting for an explanation.

"I don't think he's coming," she said. "I'll go up and change clothes now." More than anything else, she wanted to be alone.

"Just who is this young man?" her father thundered.

"I told you his name, Dad," Kathy reminded him. "Gordon Kelly."

"I've got half a mind to call his parents and find out what sort of ill-mannered slob they raised."

"You'd really have half a mind if you did that," Mrs. Price chided. "His parents aren't responsible for his bad behavior. He's old enough to take responsibility for himself."

Kathy went upstairs while her parents were still arguing. She knew her mother would succeed in keeping her father from calling the Kelly house. It occurred to her that perhaps her father was as hurt and embarrassed as she was, and the only way he could relieve his frustration was with Papa Bear-type threats. She loved both her parents fiercely, and the emotion was mixed with gratitude and relief. Somehow, all this would be forgotten, she told herself. What was that funny thing Grandma always said when something went wrong? Oh, yes.

In a hundred years, who will know the difference?

Kathy looked at herself in her mirror. In a hundred years, I'm afraid I'll still remember what it felt like to be stood up on my first date, she thought, and then her gray eyes filled with tears. If this is what dating is like, she thought helplessly, I don't think I want any part of it.

She lay down on her bed and yanked a pillow under her head. She could hear the drone of the television downstairs, and the occasional indignant rumble of her father's voice, smoothed over immediately by a soft murmur from her mother. Unconsciously, Kathy curled into a ball, with her knees tucked under her chin, and at last she slept.

Later, dreamily, she heard a distant ringing. Still half-asleep, she propped herself up on one elbow. Downstairs, her father answered the phone, and she heard him demand, "Who is this?!" Anxiously, she sat up, hugging her pillow to her chest.

"Well, Kathy is too busy to come to the phone, you young twit!" she heard her father say angrily.

Oh, Dad, she thought, that won't help. Nothing will.

When her father knocked on her door, she was tempted to pretend that she was still asleep, but he opened the door an inch and whispered, "Kathy?"

"I'm awake, Dad."

"That was Gordon what's-his-name on the phone," Mr. Price said. "He told me that he had a sudden emergency. A change of plans."

Kathy lay back on the bed. "I don't care," she said. "I'm awfully tired, Dad. Good night."

Her father hesitated for a moment and then quietly closed the door.

To avoid thinking about the terrible evening that had just passed, Kathy let herself drift back to sleep. A single tear dropped to her pillow and she sighed deeply.

Chapter 8

The talent show auditions were held the following week in the drafty school auditorium. Mr. King and three other teachers sat in the front row, while the students waiting their turns were scattered throughout the large, dimly lighted room. Kathy and Andy sat together in the back, watching the other students as they nervously stepped forward when their names were called, climbed the steps to the stage, and stood in the spotlight.

Mr. King had explained that no selections would be made until the following day, so the participants had to leave the stage without knowing whether they had succeeded or failed.

When Kathy and Andy were called, she froze in her seat and would have stayed there if Andy had not grasped her firmly by the hand and pulled her to her feet. It seemed to her that she scarcely had time to draw a breath before they were on the stage, with the spotlight blinding them. A hundred eyes watched in the dark auditorium, so she stood tall and smiled as confidently as she could.

Andy pulled a stool out from the wings and centered it on the stage, then put his foot on the lower rung and patted the seat encouragingly. Kathy sat down, and Andy strummed the first bars. Strangely, it seemed that their song was over in an instant. She listened to the last of Andy's music die away, and then felt him take her hand again and lead her down the steps.

"We made it," he whispered in her ear.

"How do you know? I was terrible."

"I just know," he said. "We made it."

Marcie and Deb were waiting outside in the hall, and as soon as the girls saw Kathy, they rushed over to her. "We could hear you out here!" Marcie cried. "You were wonderful!"

"You were the best!" Deb said as she hugged both Kathy and Andy.

"I told you so." Andy grinned. "We really were the best."

But Kathy was too nervous to appreciate their confidence. "Let's get out of here," she told them. "I need to stuff myself with something fattening."

"Yea for everything fattening!" Marcie cried. "We'll even let Andy go with us, if he pays his own way."

Andy slung his guitar over his shoulder. "Ladies, today the treat's on me. Never let it be said that Andy Andrews doesn't know how to celebrate."

As they left the school, Kathy said, "I hope you all aren't too upset when the talent show cast is posted on the bulletin board and we're not on it."

"We're going to be on it!" Andy shouted. "If you don't stop worrying about nothing, you're going to drive me crazy!"

They all piled into Andy's car, and within moments Kathy had forgotten her nervousness and was laughing with the rest of them.

"Tell 'em about Liz," Andy prompted her. "Tell 'em about that awful trio of hers."

Kathy sobered, thinking of Deb in the backseat, but Andy did not wait for her to collect her thoughts. "Boy, were they terrible," he went on. "Old Half Tone Harper and two of her tin-ear friends tried to sing without accompaniment. They sounded like brakes that need relining."

"We heard," Deb said with a giggle. "I was hoping I wouldn't have to be the one to say it. They were awful. I feel sorry for them."

"Sorry! Ha!" Andy cried. "The people in the audience were the ones who suffered!"

Wisely, Kathy said nothing. In the days that had passed

since Gordon had stood her up, she had seen Liz many times, and each time the smile on the spiteful girl's face had been strangely triumphant. Kathy had expected her to gloat publicly about the disastrous night, but Liz had said nothing. Gordon had avoided Kathy, apparently not even willing to meet her eyes. Once she had seen Gordon and Liz standing in a corner under the stairs, talking together urgently. Gordon looked angry and frustrated, but Liz was smiling proudly. The thought crossed Kathy's mind that Gordon's change of plans and urgent business probably had involved Liz, but she did not voice the thought to her friends, and Marcie and Deb never mentioned that night again after they both expressed their disgust with Gordon.

I can survive anything, Kathy had told herself, and she held her head up proudly on the first days, prepared for teasing and laughter. She was certain everyone knew what had happened, but as the days passed, no one commented on her having been stranded by Gordon and Kathy began to relax.

While they were waiting for their orders to be served in the little restaurant, Marcie, Deb, and Andy chattered happily, but Kathy lost track of their conversation. If Andy and I are chosen for the talent show, she thought, it will make up for what happened. He's so good, he'll make me sound good, too. If we're successful, maybe everyone will forget that "prep school" and "frog princess" business. Maybe they'll even forget that Gordon stood me up and doesn't even seem to be sorry about it.

A hand waved in front of her face. "Hey!" Andy said. "Are you in there? Our food arrived."

Kathy laughed and looked around. "Sorry! I was day-dreaming."

"You were planning what you're going to wear in the talent show!" Marcie accused. "You know you're going to be chosen."

"We'll find out tomorrow," Kathy said. "I'll worry about what to wear then."

"We have an extra clown suit in the drama department," Andy suggested.

"No!" Marcie and Deb cried in unison.

"But why not?" Kathy asked suddenly. "Just think about it. We're singing a sad sort of song. What if we dressed up as clowns, and put on sad clown makeup? You know what I mean, don't you, Andy?"

Andy waved his spoon enthusiastically, and the girls were liberally sprinkled with strawberry syrup. "She's a genius! It would be perfect!"

"It would be terrible!" Marcie argued. "Kathy just wants to hide from everyone, and clown makeup would do it. No! I vote that she wears a long dress."

Deb nodded seriously. "She's right. Everyone will have had enough of the clowns from the night before. You could wear clown costumes in the spring music concert, but not this time."

Kathy's ice cream was melting while the argument raged. "What spring concert? Once will be enough!"

"There's never enough," Andy insisted. "But maybe they're right. A lot of the same people will be there for the talent show, and they'll probably be tired of the clowns. So you wear a long dress and I'll wear my old brown bathrobe with the sleeves cut off and rubber boots."

They laughed helplessly at his foolishness, and the other people in the restaurant laughed along with them without knowing the reason for it. Kathy thought that her friends were wonderful, and that she was lucky to know them.

Andy reached out one arm and hugged her, almost suffocating her. While Marcie and Deb concentrated on their ice cream, Andy whispered quickly in her ear, "You'll show 'em all, prep school. You're gonna knock 'em dead, and old Gordon will wish he hadn't blown the only chance I hope he ever gets."

Kathy nodded firmly. "That was the only chance," she murmured.

"Hi!"

They all looked up at once to find Kevin standing beside their table. "How did it go?" he asked, looking at Kathy and Andy.

"We're going to be chosen for the talent show," Andy declared.

"You don't know that yet!" Kathy protested. She wondered if Kevin had seen Andy hugging her. Probably, she thought dismally. What awful luck!

"Sit down with us, Kevin," Andy invited. "It's my treat. We're celebrating in advance."

Kevin took an empty chair from the next table and put it between Marcie and Deb. "Thanks. I've got a half hour before I have to be at work today." He ordered, leaning comfortably back in his chair.

He always looks wonderful, Kathy thought. Kevin was wearing a bulky fisherman's sweater made of soft white wool. If Andy had worn it, he would have looked like a polar bear. She smiled to herself at the thought.

"What's the grin for?" Kevin asked her.

She shook her head. "It's nothing." Every time he spoke to her she blushed, and she knew that if she didn't stop, he'd know how she felt.

Kevin didn't press her. When his order came he reached out for it, and the silver ring he wore caught the light. She knew he was watching her, so she concentrated on her ice cream. He and Andy talked about Mr. King and the choir, while the girls discussed what Kathy should wear to the talent show, in spite of her protests. A half hour passed quickly, and Kevin stood up, excusing himself. His eyes caught Kathy's and he smiled at her. "You're going to make it," he assured her. "You'll see." He was gone before she could reply.

"He's so cute he makes me dizzy," said Marcie. She scraped her plate noisily. "If he smiled at me the way he smiles at you, Kathy, I'd be in a coma for weeks."

"We'd never notice," Andy said cheerfully. "Do you want to eat the plate, O dainty one, or shall I order you a second helping?"

Marcie pushed the plate away. "No thanks, big spender. We're having takeout food tonight, and I plan to leave room for seconds, thirds, and leftovers. Mom is visiting my aunt, so we can eat without fearing for our lives."

Andy dug through his pockets and pulled out a handful of crumpled bills. "I like your mom," he said thoughtfully as he put a tip for the waitress on the table. "The only mistake she ever made was not wiring your jaws shut."

They left then, and Andy drove Deb back to the school where her car was parked. Marcie decided to ride with Deb, leaving Kathy alone with Andy. He was good company and babbled cheerfully the whole way home, but when he stopped his car in front of her house, he sobered.

"I'm glad I have a chance to be alone with you," he said. "There's been something I wanted to say, but the right time never came along."

Chilled, Kathy tried to smile. Something in his tone warned her, and the afternoon's fun faded away.

"Liz heard that Gordon had asked you out," Andy continued. "She went to his house. I don't know exactly what happened, but I do know that she persuaded him to stay home with her. They're going to the Beaux Arts Ball together."

"I thought she was going with someone else? What about that boy?"

Andy shrugged eloquently. "She backed out. It looks like she and Gordon are getting back together. I wanted you to know that they're going to the ball so you'll have time to think over whether you want to go with me. I'll be playing with my band, so you'll be by yourself, and even though there are always a lot of guys who go alone, you still might not have the best time. You can change your mind about going if you want to. I probably shouldn't have asked you, anyway, because maybe you'd rather go with someone else."

Kathy thought of Kevin and pushed the thought away. It was hopeless. "No one else has asked me," she replied quietly. "And no one is going to. If you still want me to go, then that's what I want to do. I don't mind just watching the dancing, and I really want to hear your band. It's okay, Andy," she said, and she reached out her hand and touched his. "I know I'll have a good time."

"Not if Liz has anything to do with it," he declared. "I can't be with you and make music at the same time. Are you sure you don't want to think about it?"

Kathy shook her head. "I don't need to think about it." She opened the car door and swung her legs out. "But thanks for the warning. I'm not scared of Liz, and I won't be lonely."

She stood at the curb, watching him drive away. It was good of him to warn her, but she wasn't going to stay home just because Liz and Gordon were going to the ball together. They can't hurt me, she thought. I'm not the one who did something wrong. It was Gordon, and he's the one who should be embarrassed, even if he isn't.

Her mother called to her from the porch, and she turned and walked up the driveway, which was now blanketed with leaves from the maple trees. "How did the audition turn out?" her mother asked. "I've been so excited I could hardly stand it."

Kathy explained that Mr. King was not going to announce the participants in the talent show until the next day, and her mother sighed with disappointment.

"I don't know how I can stand the suspense," she said.

Kathy grinned at her sympathetically. "I don't, either. It's going to be the longest night of my life."

The next day the list of talent show participants was posted on the bulletin board outside the choir room between second and third periods. Kathy knew she and Andy had been chosen before she got close enough to the list to read it.

She was standing at the edge of the crowd, hoping that she could see the list before the bell rang. She didn't want to be late to her history class, but she was certain she could not bear to wait nearly an hour before finding out whether or not she and Andy had been accepted.

Pris Burke rudely pushed her way through the students

standing closest to the bulletin board, looked at the list, and then shoved her way back through the crowd to where Kathy was waiting patiently.

"I think it's just rotten!" she cried shrilly. "It's not fair that you were chosen when Liz wasn't! Why don't you go back to that snob school you came from!"

Kathy stepped back, shocked at Pris's vicious expression, and it took a moment before she understood all that Pris had said to her.

"You don't deserve it!" Pris raged. "I hope you get stood up again!"

She rushed away then, leaving Kathy speechless behind her. A girl Kathy barely knew smiled shyly at her and said, "Congratulations!" and several other students smiled. Kathy found herself standing in front of the list at last, and there, in Mr. King's square writing, she saw her name and Andy's, first in the column. Her breath caught in her throat. We did it! We really did it!

"I told you that you'd be chosen," she heard, and she turned around quickly to find Kevin smiling down at her. Andy was standing beside him, bouncing happily.

"We made it!" he shouted, and he threw his arms around Kathy and kissed her on the cheek, then turned and grasped Kevin's hand. "We made it!" he shouted again.

But Kathy was looking straight into Kevin's eyes, and when Andy bounced away, happy as a puppy, she didn't notice. Kevin was saying something, and she blinked. "What?"

"I said the bell is going to ring. You're going to be late to class."

The bell rang just as he finished speaking and they both laughed. "I don't care," she said suddenly, happily. She had seen Kevin's face flush a little when he looked at her, and she forgot Pris's rudeness. She even forgot the thrill of finding out that she and Andy had been chosen for the talent show.

He likes me, she told herself, looking up at him again. I know he does.

"I'll see you later," she said, and hurried away, dizzy with pleasure.

"You bet you will," she heard him say warmly.

Her footsteps echoed in the empty hall, reminding her that she was late to class. Well, thank goodness it isn't trig and Miss Correy, she thought, as she mentally prepared the apology she would offer the history teacher.

Chapter 9

Deb stared at her cottage cheese with loathing. "Why do I do this to myself? The truth is I hate dieting and I hate cottage cheese. It looks like—"

"Stop!" Marcie screamed. "Don't start describing things again. The last time you did that I couldn't eat for hours. If you don't want it, just eat your cake, but spare us your descriptions."

Deb shoved her salad plate away after offering it to Kathy. "I'd like to eat a real meal. We could stop off somewhere after we take Kathy around to all the dress shops this afternoon. Maybe we could go to Marciano's for pasta."

Marcie popped the last bite of rice into her mouth. "Great idea. There wasn't enough tomato in this stuff to satisfy me. Marciano's starts serving dinner at four, so we'll be there as soon as they open."

Kathy looked suspiciously at Marcie's plate. "Did that stuff have a name? I never saw anything that looked worse."

"I have. Every night at home," Marcie responded with a grin. "No, seriously, it's called Port Borden High Pep Rally Deluxe."

"You're kidding," Kathy said disgustedly. She finished her salad quickly and searched through her purse until she found her wallet. "I hope I didn't spend all my allowance."

"Dinner's on us," Deb announced. "We said we'd take you out to celebrate, and this is the time for it. Maybe we'll find the right dress for you today, too, even though this town isn't exactly New York. Then we'll have a double reason to celebrate."

Marcie held her hands in the air dramatically, sketching Kathy's figure. "I see you in black satin, with a slit in the skirt clear up to your hip."

"You may see it but my parents won't," Kathy replied. "I'm to choose something simple, Mom said, and she'll go by the store tomorrow and pay for it if she approves."

Deb made a face. "Gee, I hope she isn't like my mom. I always end up looking like Little Bo Peep when she chooses my clothes. She said I could have a new dress for Liz's party, as long as the dress is pink and has long sleeves."

Marcie laughed. "I'll bet. Long sleeves!"

Deb finished her cake and stacked her plates on the tray. "Well, maybe not that bad, but it's bad enough. I asked Tom to take me to the party, and he said he would, but only if he can go in his sweat shirt and those awful old jeans you sewed the patches on."

The girls stood up and carried their trays to the counter. "You're lucky that's the worst he's threatened to do," Marcie said. "You know he doesn't like parties and he's only going because he thinks you're perfect."

Deb blushed. "Well, I'll wait until he tells me that. Meanwhile he promised to go and that's enough for me right now. I was afraid he'd refuse. He doesn't like Liz very much."

Marcie said nothing and Kathy shrugged, hoping her face didn't give her thoughts away. "You'll have a good time," she said, "even if you do have to wear a pink dress with long sleeves."

Deb hurried to her next class, leaving Marcie and Kathy outside the door of their trig class. "I don't need to tell you that I wasn't invited," Marcie said with a broad grin.

"Neither was I. In fact, I didn't even know Liz was going to have a party until Deb mentioned it. I suppose everyone in the school is going except us."

"Well, Andy wasn't invited," Marcie said, "but you could have guessed that."

Kathy nodded, but she was thinking of Kevin. Had he been invited? "When is this party?"

"It's this Saturday night. And next week there's the music festival, the talent show, and the ball. But don't get the idea that we have this big a social life all the time. Actually, Port Borden probably died fifty years ago but no one noticed."

They took their seats in trig, and Marcie immediately pulled out her textbook and began checking her answers. Kathy put her book and notebook on her desk, without opening either one. She had stayed up until after midnight the night before, with both her parents helping her, and she was certain that her homework answers were correct. But she doubted that she could come up with the same answers again if she were asked to do so. The harder she tried, the more the subject eluded her, and her father had suggested that her tension had created a negative attitude toward math.

"You're right about that," she had admitted. "I have the most negative attitude in the whole world. I hate trig and it hates me."

She looked out the classroom window at the row of poplars lining the street. The trees glowed like tall flames against the brilliant autumn sky, and occasionally a shower of leaves fell in the still air.

Kevin was surely invited to Liz's party, but would he go? She wanted to ask him but knew she couldn't. Even hinting about it was more than she could bring herself to do, for just as she resented being manipulated by others, she believed that her friends felt the same way. He doesn't belong to me, she told herself. He can do as he pleases.

But she hoped desperately that he had refused Liz's invitation, for she did not like the thought of sitting home on Saturday night, wondering where he was.

Miss Correy entered the room then and Kathy gave her attention to the teacher. She caught a glimpse of Gordon from the corner of her eye. He faced straight ahead, as he always did.

You're nothing compared to Kevin, Kathy thought. I can sure live without you.

Kevin walked her from botany to choir and talked about his work with silver. He did not mention the party or Liz, and Kathy tried to concentrate on what he was saying, but she longed to hear him say that he had been asked to the party and had refused because he had to work. Or was busy with his hobby. Or best of all, because he wanted to take her to a movie instead.

They parted at the choir room door, and she did not have a chance to talk to him alone again that day.

Deb drove Marcie and Kathy to the shopping district as soon as school was out, and the three of them toured several small dress shops quickly. Kathy had seen nothing that she liked, although Marcie had been attracted to a thin black gown that would have revealed Kathy's shoulders and much more. "Mom would kill me," she said simply, and Marcie reluctantly put the dress back on the rack. "Mine, too," she admitted. "But I can always dream."

Deb led them to a department store, telling Kathy that she had often found nice clothes there when she'd had the patience to go through dozens of unsuitable things. And it was there that Kathy found the perfect dress.

It was made of a silky, opaque fabric, pale-coral and faintly shimmering under the store lights. The skirt flared out from her hips and fell in glowing folds around her. The top hugged her slender form closely, and the thin straps crossed in the back.

"Don't put on the jacket," Marcie begged when she saw Kathy in the dress, but Kathy slipped on the thin chiffon jacket and smiled wryly. "I think, if I want this dress, I'd better wear the jacket," she said.

"It's gorgeous," Deb pronounced. "The color is great on you, with that perfect skin and blond hair. And the jacket will keep Mr. King from having a coronary. Have them put it aside for you. Your mom's going to love it."

The clerk took the dress away, promising to hold it for Mrs. Price's inspection, and Kathy dressed while the other girls waited. I did look nice, she told herself. If I had looked for a week, I couldn't have found a better dress. And it's not expensive. Now if I can just keep from dying of fright that night!

Deb and Marcie took her to Marciano's after Kathy called home to report her success to her mother. "You're going to like the dress," she assured her mother. "But you sound awful. Are you catching a cold?"

"I feel terrible," Mrs. Price said. "But don't worry. I'll get the dress tomorrow. Now you go and have a good time with your friends. Your dad is going to heat some soup for our dinner and then I'm going straight to bed."

At the restaurant, the girls lingered at their table long after they had finished eating, and Mr. Marciano, who was a friend of Marcie's, brought them ice cream in little pastry shells as an extra dessert for his "favorite customer and her beautiful friends."

"Marcie is the favorite customer of every restaurant in town," Deb said after he left. "I don't know why she doesn't get fat. She deserves it."

"If I had a steady boyfriend, I probably would. That's the way life is," Marcie replied.

"You mean if you ever start going with Gordon, we'll have to save an extra seat for you in the lunchroom," Kathy snickered.

"Don't be silly," Marcie said flatly.

"Don't you like him anymore?" Deb asked curiously.

"I'll be crazy about him until the day I die," Marcie responded flippantly. "But I'm not crazy enough to go out with him. Let Liz sit around waiting for him to show up."

Deb laughed suddenly and choked on her pastry. "She doesn't wait for him, silly. She calls him up and threatens to tell his mother everything he's ever done wrong. That gets him moving."

The three girls laughed uproariously. "It's true!" Deb gasped. "She really does."

"Oh, stop!" Marcie begged. "That's awful, but he deserves it."

"They deserve each other," Kathy said suddenly, and the other two girls looked at her sharply.

"Well, it's about time you showed a little spunk!" Marcie cried.

Cautiously, Kathy looked at Deb to see if she was offended for her friend Liz's sake, but Deb was flushed from laughter. "Can you see what would happen if they ended up married?" Deb asked. "Poor Gordon. He'd have his nagging mother on one side and Liz on the other."

"And he'd still be late for everything," Marcie added.

Later, on the way home, Kathy thought that the ghost of that embarrassing evening, when she had been stood up, had finally been laid to rest. She felt safe enough to confide in her friends. "You know who I like?" she asked impulsively. "Kevin Wade."

"You and everybody else," Deb said casually.

Kathy knew that it was probably true, but she didn't like hearing Deb say it aloud.

"He never takes anyone out," Marcie provided as reassurance.

"Well, you'd know if he did," Deb said. "Does anything go on in that school that you don't know?"

"If I miss something, Andy fills me in," Marcie replied with a pleased grin, and the other girls laughed.

Kevin isn't taking anyone else out, Kathy thought exultantly. Not Liz, not anyone. When she got out of the car, she called out her good-byes happily. The afternoon had been a pleasure from beginning to end.

Mrs. Price picked up Kathy's dress the next day, and it hung in a garment bag in Kathy's closet, where she could look at it half a dozen times every day. The music festival and talent show were only ten days away, and while she would be wearing the beautiful coral dress to the talent show, Kathy and her mother considered the festival important enough to plan carefully what she would wear. Finally they settled on the simple white knit dress Kathy had worn at Christmas the winter before, so Mrs. Price pressed it and hung it next to the evening dress.

Each day Mrs. Price's head cold grew worse, and on Saturday she told Kathy and Mr. Price that she planned to spend the whole day in bed. They could hear her sneezing while they were in the kitchen, cleaning up after their dinner, and Mr. Price decided then that he should go to the pharmacy for cold medication.

"But she said she didn't want anything except hot tea," Kathy reminded him. "You know how she is about taking medication."

Mr. Price removed the apron he had been wearing and tossed it to a chair. "I don't think even a gallon of hot tea will help that cold. I'm going up now to tell her that she's sneezed enough for ten people, then I'll go to the drugstore. Maybe I can find some of that great stuff we gave you that time when you were little and had such an awful cold."

Kathy groaned dramatically. "Oh, please!" she begged. "Not that terrible black stuff! I'll never forget how bad it tasted. I got well just so I wouldn't have to take it anymore."

"That was great medicine!" Mr. Price protested. "Your grandmother gave it to me when I was a little boy."

"And look what happened. Your hair turned gray." Kathy laughed. "No, you ask Mr. Wade for something that tastes good."

"You know the pharmacist?"

Kathy shook her head. "No, but I know his son. I'm sure something has been discovered by now that will help a cold and not make Mom gag."

Her father looked doubtful, but he said, "Why don't you come along, then? You can help me decide, although it seems to me—"

"No yucky black stuff!" Kathy interrupted firmly. "I'll go up and tell Mom we're going to be gone for a few minutes." She folded the dish towel and hung in on the rack.

Kevin won't be there tonight, she thought. He probably asked for a night off so he could go to Liz's party.

She had not had the courage to mention the party to Kevin when they had walked together in the halls at school that week. As she climbed the stairs to her mother's room, she admitted to herself that she had been afraid to ask him if he was going. Even though Liz and Gordon seemed to have resumed their relationship, it was clear to Kathy that the green-eyed girl was interested in Kevin. She invented a dozen ways to attract his attention in botany and choir, and often she walked directly behind them when Kevin and Kathy were moving down the hall together. At those times her voice would ring out clearly over the chatter of the other students as she laughed with her select group of friends. Oh, yes, Kevin was probably at her house tonight, Kathy thought. But feeling bad about it wasn't going to change anything.

Mrs. Price lay propped up on pillows, watching a small portable television set. She coughed as Kathy entered the room, and Kathy frowned sympathetically.

"There's nothing good on TV tonight," Mrs. Price said crossly. "You'd think that since I have to be in bed, I could find something to watch that wasn't either depressing or boring."

Kathy laughed good-naturedly. "Nothing is fun if you have a cold. How about a book? Or one of the new magazines?"

Mrs. Price slid down on the pillows and sneezed. "Oh, no," she groaned. "Every time I sneeze, my eyes blur. I wish I could sleep."

"Dad and I are going to the drugstore to talk to the pharmacist. He'll think of something that will make you feel a little better."

Mrs. Price gestured toward the cup and teapot on her bedside table. "I'd rather have more tea."

But Kathy was firm. "There are times when it's all right to take medication, Mom, and this is one of them. Home remedies are great, but right now you need a little more help. The pharmacist will know what to do."

Mrs. Price groped for tissues and blew her nose miserably. "It's all in my mind," she said.

"Really?" Kathy asked with mock astonishment. "I thought it was in your nose."

Both of them laughed then and Kathy waved good-bye. "We'll be right back."

While she got her coat from the hall closet, her father ran upstairs to say good-bye to his wife, then ran back down again, full of self-importance, and Kathy couldn't help grinning. He was taking the business of being a full-time father and husband seriously, even though she suspected that his protective attitude might become a small problem if he kept it up too long.

The drugstore was nearly deserted, and they headed for the pharmacy counter as soon as they entered. Kathy had expected to find an older man resembling Kevin working there, but instead, a young, attractive woman greeted them. Mr. Price explained his wife's problem, and the young pharmacist listened attentively, then led him to a shelf where nonprescription cold remedies were stacked.

"Pick something that doesn't taste like old tennis shoes," Kathy reminded him.

Quick laughter burst out behind her and she turned to find Kevin standing there. He was wearing a light-blue jacket like the one worn by the clerk at the checkout stand. The white turtleneck shirt he wore under it contrasted well with his dark complexion, and Kathy's heart skipped a beat.

"I shouldn't laugh," he apologized quickly. "Aren't you feeling well?"

"I'm fine, but Mom has a cold," Kathy said. She saw her father out of the corner of her eye, watching Kevin suspiciously and evidently not listening to what the pharmacist was saying. Hastily, Kathy introduced Kevin to her father, and she was relieved at the change of expression in Mr. Price's face while he shook hands with Kevin.

The young pharmacist waited patiently until Mr. Price returned his attention to her. Kevin and Kathy moved away a few feet. She regretted having left the house in her oldest jeans and a faded shirt, but she had not expected Kevin to be there.

"Do you work here every night?" she asked, knowing the answer already but unable to think of anything else to say.

"Every night until nine, except Sunday," he said. "But I can usually get a night off now and then. My mom works here until I get out of school." He inclined his head toward the pharmacist. "That's my sister Nancy."

Kathy turned and looked at the young woman who was still explaining the various cold remedies to her father. Now she saw the resemblance. Her dark hair curled just like Kevin's and her eyes, behind metal-framed glasses, were amber.

"She's awfully pretty," Kathy commented.

"Her husband thinks so," said Kevin. "But I think of her as just my bossy big sister. I have a baby sister, too. Well, she's not exactly a baby. She's seven, and really spoiled by the rest of us. She's the reason Mom doesn't work here past three o'clock. She likes to be home when Peggy gets out of school."

Kathy took in all this information with a surge of pleasure. She hadn't known he had sisters! He so rarely spoke of himself that Kathy was practically speechless at seeing him open up like this. The only reply she could think of was, "I wish I had a sister."

Her father made a selection from among the bottles and boxes. He handed a bottle of bright-red liquid to Nancy, and when she went to the cash register, he turned to Kathy. "I hope this will be all right," he said. "They stock that good old stuff, too, but she didn't recommend it as highly."

Kathy put her hand on her father's arm. "I'm sure Kevin's sister knows best."

Mr. Price looked at Kevin approvingly. "She said you were her brother. Are you going to be a pharmacist, too?"

"No," Kevin replied. "I'll be going to the University of Washington next year to study architecture."

Mr. Price nodded thoughtfully. "That's a good choice, too. I wish Kathy had some plans for herself."

"I have plenty of time to decide," Kathy protested.

Nancy joined them then, handing Mr. Price a small sack. She looked at Kathy seriously through her neat glasses and then said to her brother, "Kevin, you can leave now if you like. We probably won't have many more customers before closing." She smiled at Kathy and returned to her place behind the counter.

There was a small awkward silence, and then Kevin said suddenly, "Mr. Price, would it be all right if I took Kathy out for a hamburger? If she wants to go, that is."

Kathy held her breath, too surprised to speak. Her father thought for a moment, then nodded his head. "But you won't keep her out late, will you?"

"No, sir," Kevin assured him. He looked down at Kathy then. "Would you like to go?"

"Oh, yes!" she breathed happily. "I'd love it." But then she remembered her mother. "Dad, do you think it's all right, with Mom sick?"

"She only has a cold, Kathy," Mr. Price said. "I think she can spare you for an hour or two." He shook hands with Kevin again and told them to enjoy themselves. Kathy watched him leave the store, and she was flushed with excitement. Kevin hadn't gone to Liz's party! He was taking her, Kathy Price, out. What luck! she thought. If she hadn't come along with her father, she would have spent another lonely Saturday night at home. She turned to face Kevin, and as she did, she caught a glimpse of herself in one of the large mirrors that lined the walls of the store. She had forgotten her awful clothes.

"I can't go like this!" she cried. "I look terrible."

Kevin smiled his delicious slow smile. "You look good to me. I thought that when you came in."

Kathy blushed under his scrutiny.

"Wait here," he said. "I'll hang up my jacket in the back room and then we'll go."

She nodded. She wouldn't have left the pharmacy then

if it had been on fire. She looked at her reflection again, and she saw a small, slender, pretty girl whose bright eyes and blushing cheeks told the world she was happier than she had ever been.

Chapter 10

"Tell me about it again," Marcie demanded the next day. "Tell me every single thing and don't leave anything out."

They were sitting in Marcie's beautiful bedroom, stuffing themselves on the fudge they had made earlier under the watchful but inexpert eye of Marcie's mother. Everywhere Kathy looked, she saw the results of Mrs. Clark's skill with a needle, from the crisp yellow curtains to the lovely flowered quilt. Even the rugs had been hooked by the talented woman.

Kathy licked her lips. "I told you everything, which is practically nothing. We went to that hamburger place on the highway..."

"Derrie's," Marcie supplied. "That's the most expensive hamburger place in town."

"Derrie's," Kathy agreed. "And I don't remember what my hamburger tasted like, so don't ask. I think my taste buds died of fright before we got there."

"I can't imagine anything like that happening, but go on. What did he say and what did you say?"

"How do I know? I was delirious, or something. We talked. I think he said something about botany. Or maybe I did. Anyway, we ate and then he took me home."

"And?" Marcie urged.

"And nothing! My father opened the door the minute my foot touched the porch steps," Kathy said. "You would have had to be there to believe it. I think he was peeking out the window. Anyway, he opened the door and said, 'Thanks for bringing her home early, Kevin.'"

"Oh, no!" Marcie breathed.

"Oh, yes. And Kevin said, 'You're welcome, sir.'"

"And that was it?" Marcie cried. "Tell me it isn't so!"

"I'm telling you that it is. That was it! I watched Kevin drive away, and then my dad pulled me into the house and told me that I looked exhausted, so I'd better go to bed, just in case I came down with Mom's cold."

"I can't believe it. Your dad sounds as bad as mine. Well, have more fudge. It won't change anything, but it will take away some of the pain. I wish Kevin had asked you for another date."

Kathy accepted another piece of fudge and leaned back in her chair. "So do I, but he didn't. He probably was so bored with our conversation that he's sorry he took me out for the hamburger. Maybe," she speculated, "I should have offered to pay for it."

"Are you crazy?" Marcie asked seriously. "You act as if that were your first date."

Well, Kathy thought, it was, except for that rotten evening I spent waiting for Gordon to show up. "I was only joking," she said to her friend. "But don't you know what I mean? If I had it to do over, I would have practiced some clever things to say. And I would have worn something better than a shirt I've had since I was fourteen. At least I didn't have on my Micky Mouse sweater."

Marcie sighed and helped herself to the last of the fudge. "It's fate," she said. "I really believe it. Whenever we ought to look our best, we look like something that fell off the back of a salvage truck."

"Maybe he'll come to the talent show and see me in the fabulous dress."

"He would come if you asked him, I bet."

Kathy shook her head. "Well, I'm not going to. The truth is, just knowing he was in the audience would strike me tone deaf. I'm going to be scared enough as it is."

Marcie reached for the comb on her dressing table and yanked it impatiently through her short, shining hair. "You're going to be a star, and don't forget it. You'll have a chance to get the feeling of being in front of an audience the night before at the music festival, so you'll be an old pro by the time you and Andy walk onstage at the talent show."

"I sing two lines alone at the music festival," Kathy groaned. "Big deal. That hardly makes me an old pro."

"It makes you someone Liz hates more than she's ever hated anyone before!" Marcie laughed and threw herself backward on her bed, kicking her feet in the air. "You can't imagine what it does for me, to see her so bent out of shape over you getting all that attention two nights in a row. She yaps about it all the time. And just wait until she hears that you went out with Kevin on the night of her party."

Kathy stood up quickly. "You can't tell her! Promise that you won't!"

"For Pete's sake, Kathy!" Marcie sat up, sober and startled. "You act like you're afraid of her. What can she do to you now? Everyone who's heard you sing thinks you're terrific, and as soon as they all find out that Kevin took you out—"

"Please, Marcie!" Kathy implored. "I'm not kidding about this. I don't want Liz to know. She has a way of spoiling things."

"She's back with Gordon now!" Marcie protested. "What does she have to gripe about, except that Kevin obviously preferred your company to hers?"

"But she likes him. I know she does. You should see the way she looks at him in botany. I think she'd dump Gordon in a minute if she thought Kevin were interested in her."

"He's interested in you. That's obvious."

"Maybe." Kathy sat down again, miserable and worried. "Promise you won't say anything. It's very important to me. If Kevin is really interested in me, he'll ask me out again on a real date. In the meantime, I don't want Liz plotting anything. If she thinks Kevin only walks me to class, she won't pay attention to us." Kathy couldn't let Marcie know the depth of her feeling for Kevin because she was uncertain of it herself. She had never felt this way before about a boy, but she had not had much experience.

Maybe this was just puppy love. Or maybe she was what her mother called "boy crazy."

Marcie sat up and investigated the fudge plate carefully for crumbs. "Okay. I'll keep your secret, but I think you're crazy. What if Kevin tells her?"

Kathy stared at her friend for a moment, puzzled, and then she said, "I think that would be different. If he told her, I'll bet she'd just back off. But I don't think boys tell other girls things like that."

Marcie reflected on this. "Well, some boys don't. But Tom tells me who he's taking out."

"He's your brother!" Kathy protested.

"And Andy tells me, too," Marcie added.

Kathy laughed and slumped in her chair. "Andy tells everyone everything, but if he were ever seriously interested in a girl, he'd never breathe a word. He probably wouldn't even tell *her*."

They looked at each other and grinned. "I had a crush on him once," Marcie said. "In third grade. I was madly in love with him, as a matter of fact. But he never noticed, and when we came back from summer vacation I was several yards taller than he was, and he never caught up. So much for true love."

"That has to be the dumbest story you ever told," Kathy said. She dug through her purse until she found her lipstick and comb, and then seated herself at Marcie's dressing table. She could see Marcie in the mirror, and her eyes were strangely bright.

"Would I lie to you, pal?" Marcie asked with mock sincerity.

"Yes," said Kathy, and she applied lipstick with quick strokes.

"I'm not lying," Marcie declared flatly.

Kathy whirled around and faced her friend. Now Marcie's eyes swam with tears. "Stupid, isn't it?" she asked Kathy. "I'm big enough to be his bodyguard. He calls me Dainty One and Tinker Bell. He asks me how the weather is 'up there.' And he takes out teeny-tiny girls with teeny-tiny brains." A large tear rolled down her face and plopped on her shirt, staining the pale-blue fabric. When she looked down at the spot, she laughed. "Oh, Kathy, look at me. I can't even cry delicately. I'm just a big horse, like Liz says, and Andy is never going to take me seriously. Never. How can you take someone seriously when all you ever see of her is her kneecaps?"

Kathy stiffled the urge to laugh, knowing that her own hot tears would quickly follow. She sat down on the edge of the bed and patted Marcie's shoulder. "I had no idea you felt that way about him," she said. "It never occurred to me. I'm really sorry, and if there's something I can do, I wish you'd tell me. Maybe I could sort of hint to him that he ought to take another look at you."

"Why don't you just hint that the school Amazon wishes he'd take her out dancing? He'd need a chair to see if I was wearing lipstick."

"You're not that much taller. Only three little inches."

"It might as well be three little feet."

Suddenly both girls began laughing, until Tom came and banged on Marcie's door. "Let's have a little quiet, troops," he yelled   "The plaster's cracking downstairs!"

"Do you suppose he heard?" Kathy asked in a whisper.

Marcie shook her head. "No. He never hears anything unless he thinks someone is having a good time, and then he complains."

The two girls looked at each other soberly for a long time before Kathy spoke. "Sometimes life isn't a bit of fun," she said. "Sometimes I'm even sorry I'm not in kindergarten anymore."

"Tell me about it," said Marcie. "In kindergarten, Andy was taller than I was."

As Kathy walked home later in the early October dusk, she thought over Marcie's confession. When she tried to picture Marcie and Andy together, a smile pulled at the corners of her mouth. If only he were taller! But then, she thought, did it really matter so much? Andy and Marcie had many things in common. Best of all, they were loyal friends who laughed easily and often. What more could anyone want from a relationship? Wasn't real love made up of companionship as well as romance? She shook her head as she turned into her driveway. Why did everything have to be so complicated?

When she walked into the kitchen, Mrs. Price turned away from the stove and said, "Andy called you. He wants you to call him back as soon as you can."

"I'll bet he wants to rehearse another hundred times," Kathy said, but she was thinking that Marcie would have given a great deal to have received such a message.

Life wasn't only complicated, sometimes it hurt. But having good friends made everything easier, because they could share feelings.

There had been one moment, however, that Kathy had not shared with Marcie when she was telling about her date with Kevin. It had been too precious to tell. While she and Kevin had walked across the restaurant parking lot toward his car, he had caught her hand in his. She still remembered how it felt. His hand was large and strong, completely encircling hers, and his silver ring pressed against her fingers. Neither of them said a word, and when he let go of her hand to open the door for her, she had a sudden and quite silly thought. I'll never wash this hand again, she vowed childishly, and then she laughed at herself.

But now she looked down at the hand Kevin had held and wondered if he would ever hold it again.

Chapter 11

The week went by too fast, and Friday was upon her before she felt truly prepared. The entire choir was tense during sixth period, and funny Mr. King was no help to them, for he paced about, pulling at his curly hair, offering advice and support and then contradicting himself a dozen times over. In the last minute of the class, he raised his arms and shouted, "Now calm down, everybody! We're going to be just great tonight, and don't any of you forget it. Just stay calm."

Someone snickered and Mr. King laughed aloud. "You're right," he said. "I'm the worst of the lot, but do as I say and not as I do. See you all tonight."

The bell rang and the class surged toward the door. Kevin caught up with Kathy in the hall outside the class, saying, "I'm coming to the festival tonight, of course, because Mr. King would have my head if I didn't. But I can't ask for two nights off in a row, so I won't be able to see you sing at the talent show tomorrow. I didn't want you to think I didn't care about it."

Kathy studied her shoes as if they had somehow changed color since she had put them on that morning. "That's all right," she replied. "I wish none of my friends were coming to see me fall on my face."

"Don't talk like that," Kevin said seriously. "You're going to be great. But I wanted you to know how sorry I am that I won't be there. By the time I get off work, the show will be over."

And I'll be at the Beaux Arts Ball, Kathy thought miserably. She wondered if he had planned to go to the ball, but she was afraid to ask. Some boys did come without dates, she had been told. Would he be one of them?

"I've got time to take you home before I have to show up for work," Kevin said.

Kathy's heart sank. "Thanks, but Andy is making me stay after school today to rehearse one more time. We won't be through for better than an hour."

She couldn't tell from his expression whether or not he was disappointed, and all he said was, "Another time, then."

She watched him as he walked off, hoping he would turn back once to look at her, but he didn't. She walked slowly toward her locker, and when she got there, Andy was waiting, bouncing irritably up and down.

"Great Scott, woman! Why are you so slow?" he demanded. "I'll bet you were poking around under the stairs with Kevin the Magnificent."

Across the hall, Marcie began laughing, but Kathy didn't share their amusement. "I was not doing anything like that!" she cried. "Andy, sometimes you make me so mad I could punch you."

Andy leaped back, covering his head with his arms. "Help! Marcie! Protect me from this wild woman."

Kathy saw Marcie's face and knew Andy had gone too far again. Marcie was white with anger at Andy's implication that she was physically stronger than he was, although it was probably true. She slammed her locker door shut, nearly catching Bibi's hand in it. "Kathy's right!" she shouted. "You make me so mad *I* could punch you. You're silly and conceited and . . . *short!*"

With that, Marcie stormed away, not looking back, and Kathy saw that Andy's usually cheerful face was flushed with embarrassment.

"Serves you right," she said to him. "You could be a little more considerate of her. Did you ever stop to think that you might hurt her feelings with all your crummy jokes about her height? The rest of us think she's beautiful."

But Andy was watching Marcie walk away, and he did

not answer Kathy. He pushed his glasses up on his long nose and murmured, "Well, well," to himself. Then he turned to Kathy and barked, "Let's get going, prep school!"

She was not certain whether or not he meant to remind her of the hard times she had had when she'd first come to the school, but she thought it might be wise to make an effort to smooth over his ruffled feelings. "Right," she said. "And I'm sorry I was late."

She accompanied him to the auditorium, where they had permission to rehearse, and decided not to mention to him that she felt she was coming down with a cold. This was definitely not the time to give him any cause for concern, and anyway, her throat was only a little bit sore.

That's all I need, she thought. A cold like Mom's.

By the time she was dressing for the music festival that evening, her throat was too sore to ignore, so her father went to the drugstore for another consultation with Nancy, Kevin's sister. When he returned, he brought with him a throat spray Nancy said would give Kathy temporary relief, but she recommended that Kathy see a doctor the next morning.

Kathy tried the spray and pronounced it absolutely disgusting. "It's like the black stuff," she complained to her mother. "Only it's green. Yuck."

Mrs. Price was making a last-minute adjustment to the waistline of the white knit dress while Kathy was wearing it. "We'll take you to the doctor first thing in the morning. We can't have you sick tomorrow night. Are you sure you don't have a fever?"

Kathy looked past her mother at the mirror on her bedroom door. "No, I took my temperature again just a few minutes ago. It's normal, and I don't feel too bad. It's just that my throat is scratchy." She fluffed up her hair with nervous fingers.

"You sound a little stuffed up," Mrs. Price commented as she clipped off a loose thread from Kathy's dress.

"Oh, no!" Kathy explained. "Is it bad?"

"No, and let's hope you don't get any worse before we

get you to the doctor." Mrs. Price stepped back and looked at Kathy appraisingly. "You look absolutely beautiful. That lipstick is the right color, too. I know you were worried about it being too dark, but I don't think it is. We're so proud of you, Kathy."

Mr. Price stopped in the open doorway and echoed his wife. "And both of my ladies look wonderful tonight," he added. "But if you two have plans about showing up on time, I think we'd better get started. It's almost seven o'clock, and the program starts in half an hour."

They hurried for their coats then, and minutes later, they arrived at the school auditorium. Kathy ran backstage to join the other choir members, and her parents found seats near Deb's parents in the second row. Kathy looked through an opening in the curtains and restrained the urge to wave to them. The parents of all the choir members were there, and she wondered which ones were Kevin's.

When she walked away from the curtain, she saw Kevin, tall and handsome in a dark-blue suit. He was talking to Andy, who looked a little less like a bear in his dark-gray suit. Deb pushed past them then, to compliment Kathy on her dress. Deb was wearing a pink dress with elbow-length sleeves, and Kathy suspected that this was the dress her mother had chosen for her to wear to Liz's party. It looked lovely on Deb, and Kathy told her so, but Deb wrinkled her nose.

"I bet Mom borrows it from me for her fiftieth-anniversary party," she said. "I hate this dress, but the one I'm wearing tomorrow is worse."

Kathy smiled sympathetically and would have said something, but at that moment Liz pushed between her and Deb, keeping her back to Kathy, and interrupted their conversation. She was wearing a pale-green silk dress that showed off her red hair, and Kathy would have commented on it had Liz not been so rude.

"Are you going with us after the festival is over?" Liz demanded of Deb. "We're all going out for something to eat and then on to my place for some dancing."

"Sure," Deb said. "Sounds like fun."

Liz moved along then, deliberately avoiding Kathy's eyes, and behind her, Pris Burke grinned maliciously at Kathy, her thin lips stretched over her prominent teeth. When the two of them disappeared in the crowd, Deb said, "I'd rather go home and watch TV, but I'd hear about it for the rest of my life. You aren't missing anything. Liz's dances are a drag."

Kathy shrugged. "She didn't hurt my feelings. Sooner or later she'll give up trying."

But she was looking past Deb, to where Kevin stood, taller than those around him. He was talking to someone, nodding and smiling, and Kathy thought she saw a flash of red hair. She's asking him, Kathy thought, and he's going to go.

Her throat began hurting her suddenly, and she swallowed hard. No, she told herself. I'm not going to let Liz ruin tonight for me.

Mr. King came in then, dressed in a suit for once, and his wild hair was neatly combed. Kathy scarcely recognized him. He clapped his hands and silence fell over the group. "Take your places, ladies and gentlemen. The show is about to begin."

Afterward, when the last note died away, Kathy looked out into the glare of the spotlights and smiled until her face hurt. The applause went on for several minutes, and she knew the choir deserved it. They filed off the stage and the orchestra took their places. Quickly, making as little noise as possible, the choir members found seats in the back of the auditorium and settled down to listen to the orchestra. During the last number, Andy and the other drama club clowns slipped out, and when intermission came, the clowns tumbled out onto the stage and put on their act.

Kathy stayed in her seat, along with several of the other choir members, and she laughed until her throat reminded her that she had better take care of it. Kevin moved to sit beside her, and once he whispered, "They're really good, aren't they? For a while I didn't think they were going to be able to get their act together, but they're as good as any clowns I've ever seen in a circus."

Unexpectedly, Liz leaned over Kevin's shoulder. She had been sitting behind Kathy, and Kathy had been ignoring the shrill voice of Pris, who had gossiped all through the orchestra's performance. "They're not as good as the clowns I saw in New York," Liz said to Kevin. "This is strictly amateur night."

The clowns tumbled off the stage then, to a burst of applause, and Kevin's answer to Liz was lost in the uproar. The lights dimmed in the auditorium again, and Kevin went back to his seat. Kathy looked over at him, wishing she could stop wondering if he were going to Liz's house.

Behind her, Liz took up a whispered conversation with Pris, and Kathy concentrated on the jazz band that came out on the stage. Andy, she saw, had changed clothes again and was playing piano for the jazz group, and she wondered if there was anything the talented boy could not do.

He can't tell when he's breaking someone's heart, she thought. Several rows ahead of her Marcie and her family were sitting together. She hoped Marcie was able to enjoy the performance. And she hoped that somehow, through what miracle she could not imagine, Andy would one day come to realize that Marcie cared about him.

The jazz band received a standing ovation, and when the lights came on, the audience began wandering out. Kathy saw her parents and waved, and Mr. Price pointed toward the lobby, where he obviously wanted Kathy to meet them as soon as she could.

She studied the parents as they walked past, wondering which were Kevin's, but there were too many people, and when she looked around, hoping to see Kevin walking toward one or another of the couples, she saw that he was gone. And so was Liz.

Kathy joined the crowd in the aisles then, and tried to keep her mind on the performance. There was no point in worrying about what she could not help, but that state of mind was not an easy one to maintain. As she moved toward her smiling parents, she wondered why it was so simple to give herself convincing advice and so hard to follow it. She *did* care where Kevin was. She cared so much that the evening was spoiled.

"Hey, frog princess!" she heard, and her head jerked around. A plump, smiling girl with long black hair caught her eye. "You did a great job tonight," the girl said, and then she was swept away in the crowd.

At first, Kathy was annoyed at the unkind nickname, but then she smiled. Probably that was the best the girl could do toward making an overture of friendship, and Kathy had to admit that she was grateful.

By the next morning Kathy's cold was no worse, but she went to a doctor anyway, and explained to him that she was to sing in the school talent show that evening. Was there any help he could give her sore throat?

There was, but Kathy said afterward that she would have preferred a whole bottle of the dreaded black stuff her father praised so much. The doctor had sprayed something in her throat that tasted awful, she told her mother, and also had given her a prescription for some tablets that would relieve her other cold symptoms.

Mrs. Price took her home and then went to the drugstore to fill the prescription. Kathy crawled into bed, wishing she could fall asleep, but was too nervous about the evening ahead to close her eyes. Mrs. Price did not return until nearly noon, and when she did she brought with her a florist's box which she put down on the bed next to Kathy. "For tonight," she explained. "I saw them and thought they would be perfect with your dress."

Kathy took off the lid and pulled back the green waxed paper that covered the flowers. A corsage of pale-yellow roses lay inside. "It's just perfect," she said. "Thanks, Mom. I never even thought of flowers."

"That's not all I got," said Mrs. Price. She went out into the hall and returned with a garment bag from the store where Kathy had bought her dress. "You don't have one, and when I saw this, I knew it would be just right."

She lifted off the plastic and showed Kathy a midnight-blue velvet evening coat, floor-length and decorated with a long line of rhinestone buttons.

Kathy leaped out of bed and reached for the coat. "It's beautiful!" she cried. "Let me try it on, right this minute."

"Over your pajamas?" Her mother laughed.

"Over anything," Kathy said firmly, and she slipped on the coat.

Her reflection looked back at her in the mirror. "I never saw anything this beautiful," she declared. "I wish I could wear it every day."

Mrs. Price took away the corsage, to store it in the refrigerator, and left Kathy standing in front of the mirror. Over and over she ran her hands across the rich velvet, and finally, reluctantly, she hung the coat back on its hanger and put it in her closet, next to the coral dress.

When she crawled back into bed, she slept until late afternoon when her mother called her to tell her that dinner was waiting. Kathy had no appetite, for in spite of the doctor's medication her cold symptoms were still with her, but she ate to please her worried parents.

Andy called twice, to reassure himself that she was going to show up, and Marcie and Deb both called to wish her luck. But when it came time for her to leave, she felt that she would need more than luck. She was so nervous that she nearly left the house without her flowers. As she passed the hall mirror, she stopped one last time to assure herself that she looked presentable.

It's going to be all right, she told herself. There's nothing to be afraid of.

But a little voice in the back of her mind kept whispering, *Look out, Kathy.*

Chapter 12

One by one the talent show acts walked out on the stage, performed, and accepted their applause. For most of the show, Kathy and Andy sat in a small room behind the stage, worrying with the other performers, but as the time for their act drew closer, they gave up trying to remain calm and stood in the wings, watching.

Three girls that Kathy knew only slightly were dancing, enacting a fairy tale, and Kathy was fascinated with their performance. She had seen them rehearsing in their faded warm-ups and had thought them to be unusually talented, but with their act perfected, and wearing lovely costumes, they were marvelous.

"Can you see the way Mr. King arranged the program?" Andy asked her in a quiet whisper. "The acts get better as they go along."

Kathy stared at him. "You mean that's why he put us last? Because he thinks we're the best?" Goose bumps broke out on her arms. She was not certain she wanted such a responsibility.

Andy nodded emphatically. "We are the best. He told me so."

"I don't believe you. You're making that up just to scare me."

The dancers finished, bowed, and ran to the wings. As they passed Kathy, she saw that they were drenched with perspiration. Immediately, they dried themselves off with towels and pulled on robes, and then they ran off to the storerooms that were being used as dressing rooms by the students who were wearing costumes.

A young magician was entertaining the audience now, but Kathy could not concentrate on him. She and Andy were next. He had already taken his guitar out of its case and disappeared for a moment while he tuned it out of the hearing of the people out front; when he returned, he looked nervous, too. The sight of him biting his lower lip did nothing to calm Kathy's fears.

He was wearing a loose, long-sleeved white shirt, open at the neck, and he had left off his glasses, giving him a completely different look. He was actually cute! But his heavy dark hair curled damply from perspiration, and she thought distractedly that if Andy was scared, who would help her relax?

But then she had no more time to worry, for the magician was bowing and smiling his thanks for the applause he was getting. When he walked toward them, he was glassy-eyed with relief.

"Break a leg," he said as he passed, and Kathy knew that was the traditional greeting performers give, instead of saying "good luck."

"We're on," Andy whispered, and he led Kathy out to the dark stage where someone had already placed their tall stool. The spotlight shone down on them just as Kathy had seated herself, and Andy waited until he had counted to five, just as he'd said he would, before he began to play. It was too late for Kathy to be afraid. It was too late to do anything but open her mouth and sing what she had rehearsed so many times.

Oddly, the scent of the roses she wore came to her while she was singing. When the song had ended, and she knew that they had done well, she stood and bowed, holding hands with Andy. Impulsively, she pulled one of the roses free from her corsage and handed it to him. The crowd went wild, and would not let them leave the stage until they had bowed a dozen times.

Her parents met her in the wings, with Marcie and Deb,

and it was several minutes before Kathy's ears stopped ringing and her excitement died down so that she could hear what they were saying to her.

Andy's parents joined them, and all of them laughed and interrupted one another until at last Mr. King came and solemnly shook hands with both Kathy and Andy.

Kathy was too dazed to think straight, and her mother had to tell her twice that she and her father were leaving and would see her after the Beaux Arts Ball was over. As soon as they had gone, Andy became impatient to leave, saying it would take his band a few minutes to set up. "Are you coming or aren't you?" he demanded.

Marcie's laugh brought Andy to a halt. "For Pete's sake, Andy, let her enjoy this for a minute! You're used to people making a big fuss over you."

Andy's quick silence was odd. He shrugged and stood back, allowing Deb and Marcie to hug Kathy once more. Marcie was carrying Kathy's evening coat, and she held it out to her.

"We'll see you at the ball," she said. "I'm going with my ugly brother and Deb in Tom's car."

"Watch it," Deb cautioned. "You know I think Tom's cute."

"I'll see you there," Kathy said. Andy was so cranky, she almost wished she were riding with them.

"You won't see them if we don't get going," Andy complained after Marcie and Deb left. "Are you finally ready? Do you want me to help you with your coat? Are mere mortals allowed to touch it?"

"No." Kathy laughed. She struggled with the coat as they made their way through the crowd. Half the student body of Port Borden High seemed to be backstage. Kathy tried to squeeze through but she had no success until Andy grabbed her arm. He was shouting directions to the other members of his band, also caught in the crowd. Behind her, Kathy could hear Liz and Pris talking with the magician. She was following Andy slowly through the crowd, heading for the exit and still trying to get her evening coat over her shoulders, when suddenly she felt a tug on the back of her dress. She looked around quickly and saw both Liz and Pris looking at her.

"Sorry," Liz said. "I guess I stepped on your dress, but it's okay."

Pris giggled, her blotchy face alive with malice, and Kathy resigned herself to having a footprint on the hem of her dress. Well, there was no time to investigate the damage now. At last she pulled the coat around her and got her arms in the sleeves, and then Andy grabbed her hand, pulling her through the door into the cold parking lot.

"Now hurry up," he said firmly. "I should have been at the civic center ten minutes ago, setting things up."

"You were onstage ten minutes ago, lapping up all the attention you were getting," Kathy argued. "Be a little reasonable, will you?"

He yanked open the car door and put his guitar in the backseat, then scurried around to the passenger side to help Kathy in. "If you had any more material in that dress and coat, I could make a tent," he complained.

Kathy retaliated with, "Will you shut up and relax?"

Andy scowled at her, then took his glasses from his pocket and put them on. "Great Scott!" he cried. "There's a whole world out there!" Kathy refused to laugh.

While they were on the way to the civic center, Andy broke their exhausted silence by saying, "You were good tonight. And you looked great, too. The dress and flowers made you look like someone on television. Did Kevin send you the roses?"

Kathy touched the corsage, moving the lapel of her coat away from it so that the petals would not be crushed. "No, my folks gave them to me." Andy could always be counted on to find a sore place and poke it, she thought.

"Well, thanks for giving me a rose. It's in my pocket. The crowd sure liked it."

"I didn't do it for the crowd, silly," Kathy told him. "I did it because you helped me so much."

Andy took one hand from the steering wheel and fished

the rose from his shirt pocket. "I'll put it in my buttonhole when we get there. And I won't forget why you did it. Sorry if I put things the wrong way. Sometimes I do that, even when I don't mean to."

"I noticed," said Kathy, thinking of Marcie.

But Andy didn't respond. He was humming the tune they had sung, and in a moment Kathy joined him. It was too nice a night to quarrel, and it was hard to stay mad at Andy. By the time they reached the civic center, Kathy had forgotten the tug she had felt on the back of her dress when she had been making her way through the backstage crowd.

Port Borden's civic center had been decorated by the high school art department, under Marcie's direction, and when Kathy walked in she gasped in astonishment. She had been inside the shabby old building once with Marcie when her friend was dropping off some decorations. She knew Marcie and the other art students had worked hard, but she never dreamed that their efforts would be so successful. The place looked completely different.

Blue and white balloons had been covered with glitter, and enormous clusters of them hung from the ceiling. Ropes of gleaming silver satin ribbon had been threaded between the balloon clusters and hung in loops on the walls, framing giant glittering white masks that reminded Kathy of the masks ancient Greek actors wore. On three sides of the room, long tables had been decorated with silver paper and heaps of autumn leaves sprayed with blue and white glitter paint. Here and there along the colored leaves, arrangements of large white flowers circled silver candles.

"It looks like something out of a dream," she said to Andy. "Did you know that Marcie designed this?"

"How could I *not* know?" he asked. "She's only been telling me every ten minutes for weeks." But he looked around approvingly. "She calls it the winter palace, so I guess I'd better go up to the bandstand and start heating things up. Are you going to be okay by yourself? You won't just sit in a corner and sulk, will you?"

Kathy laughed and twirled away from him, the evening

coat swinging out and showing the front of her beautiful gown. "I'm going to sit with Marcie and Deb, and who knows? Maybe Tom will dance with me."

"Watch your feet, then," Andy said as he walked away. "Giants have a way of stomping on us wee folk."

He joined his friends on the bandstand and Kathy wished that a giant would stomp on him, preferably Marcie. She wondered if he had any idea how much he hurt her, decided that he did not, and then dismissed him from her mind.

She saw Marcie and Deb on the other side of the room and hurried to join them. Fortunately, they had saved a place for her at one of the tables, because the seats near them were filling up fast. Kathy sat down, still wearing her coat because the room was cool, and she noticed then that Liz sat directly across the room from her, watching her. Liz was wearing another pale-green dress, this one cut so low in the front that Kathy wondered if Liz's mother were blind. Gordon, wearing a dinner jacket and looking uncomfortable, sat next to her, and he was pouring something from a small bottle into his soft drink. I might have known, Kathy thought. The more she saw of Gordon, the more grateful she was that he had stood her up. She had been attracted to him, she admitted to herself, so she could not imagine how she would have handled matters if they had gone out and then she had found out that he was stupid enough to drink at a high school dance. The table opposite the bandstand had been reserved for parents and teachers, and most of them were already present.

Well, that's his problem, she decided, and turned her attention to her friends. She had not had time before to admire the dresses Marcie and Deb were wearing, and now she examined them more closely, since both of them had removed their coats. Marcie's mother had made the pretty yellow dress Marcie wore. The top had an overlay of lace, which Marcie had said once belonged to her grandmother. The lightly gathered skirt accentuated Marcie's slim hips, and Kathy thought that she had never looked prettier. If only Andy would notice, but he was busy tuning his guitar and laughing with the band. Kathy scowled and looked at Deb.

The cute blonde, seeing Kathy's glance, said, "Isn't it awful? My mother loves Shirley Temple movies. This is her idea of fashion."

Kathy had to admit to herself that she was glad her own mother had not found the dress first. It would have been just right on a ten-year-old, and it made Deb look just that young. Layers of white ruffles hid Deb's slim figure, and Kathy was sure Deb was wearing a stiff petticoat under the dress. But Tom beamed delightedly at Deb, and Kathy decided that if Tom was so impressed with Deb's dress, who were they to criticize it? "You look like a doll I used to have," she whispered to Deb.

"Better check your toy box when you get home," Deb said grimly. "Mom didn't tell me where she found this creation."

Kathy laughed and slipped her arms out of her coat sleeves. The room had gotten more crowded and was finally beginning to warm up. Andy's band began playing, and several couples moved out to the floor to start dancing. Tom pulled Deb to her feet and they left the table.

"We're alone," Marcie said. "Two old maids withering on the vine."

"I refuse to look at it that way," Kathy replied. "And anyway, here comes Jim Abbott, and he looks like he's either going to ask you to dance or ask you to marry him. I can't decide which."

Marcie slumped in her chair. "Oh, thrill, thrill. What's the difference? Either way, it's going to be a long night."

Jim approached cautiously, looking as if Marcie had already turned him down. "Wanna dance?" he mumbled at her, and his face flamed clear to his blond hairline.

"I'd love to!" cried Marcie, and Kathy admired her acting. Marcie looked back at her once and winked. Jim would never know that he was not Marcie's first choice, and Kathy was impressed with her kindness.

But she was alone at the table now, for all the others

were dancing, so she concentrated on her popcorn and soft drink. It didn't really matter if no one asked her to dance. Nothing could spoil this evening.

Several people stopped by the table to congratulate her on her singing at the talent show, and this added to her pleasure. Two of them were Liz's friends. Perhaps things would be better at school after this. She could almost believe that soon she would fit in like Marcie and Deb.

The evening was half-over when a boy from her English class stopped at the table and shyly asked her to dance. Kathy stood up, slightly embarrassed, remembering the dances at St. Catherine's when the boys had been required to dance with the girls. She wondered if one of the teachers had seen her sitting alone and sought out one of the single boys, demanding that he ask Kathy to dance. She was tempted to refuse, but then she decided that she would be a poor sport if she did, so she took his outstretched hand and walked out on the dance floor.

They had not danced for more than a minute or two when she first heard the laughter behind her. Puzzled, the boy she was dancing with stopped and looked over her shoulder. Kathy turned, her face flushing. She was not an expert dancer, but she was not that bad, and the boy actually danced quite well. Why were the others laughing?

Pris, standing with a hawk-faced boy Kathy had seen in the halls, pointed at Kathy's skirt. Kathy looked down at it, seeing nothing wrong. Laughter erupted behind her, and she heard her dance partner swear under his breath. She looked up at him, startled. "What's wrong?" she asked.

He backed away from her, his face scarlet. A circle of Liz's friends had formed around her, and Kathy turned slowly, sick with embarrassment, while the laughter soared.

Suddenly, Deb broke through the ring of jeering students. She held Kathy's evening coat, and quickly she draped it over Kathy's shoulders. "Come on," she whispered. "Tom is taking us home. Right now."

The band faltered to a stop. Kathy stared at Deb, surprised at seeing her look so angry. "Why won't anyone tell me what's wrong?"

"Your dress is torn," Deb said quietly.

Marcie joined them, crying angrily. "I think you're all a bunch of creeps!" she shouted furiously to the group surrounding Kathy. "I hope the same thing happens to every one of you."

With Deb on one side of her and Marcie on the other, Kathy was rushed from the room, followed by sympathetic, angry friends. Tom was waiting in the parking lot.

"I don't understand what could have happened!" Kathy cried. She was pulling at the coat, trying to examine the back of her dress. "I didn't know my dress was torn."

In minutes, Tom had them at the Price house, and then told them he was returning to the dance. "I feel like knocking some heads together."

The moment they were inside the door, Kathy whipped off her coat, and with her astonished parents watching, she turned slowly in front of the hall mirror until she could see the back of her dress. It had been torn from hem to hip, and since she had not needed a slip under it, even her lace-trimmed panties were visible.

"I don't believe it," she said, stunned.

Mrs. Price bent and examined the back of the dress. "This material has been slashed with something sharp," she said in a shocked voice. "See? It's not a tear, with ragged edges. Someone cut it."

Too late, Kathy recalled when she felt the tug on her dress. "Sorry," she remembered Liz saying. "I stepped on your dress."

"It was Liz," she told them, sick with anger. "I felt a pull on my dress when she was standing behind me, and she said she had stepped on it. She even apologized for it."

Deb's face went white. "I'll bet you're right," she replied. "She and Pris were giggling about something during the talent show. I was sitting right behind them, and I heard Pris ask Liz if she had her nail scissors with her. Liz laughed and said she wasn't in the mood to give a manicure. She said she was in the mood to do another kind of clipping."

"Nail scissors!" Kathy exclaimed. "She couldn't have made a cut that long with little nail scissors!"

"Oh, yes, she could," Marcie responded. "The material is so light that she could have done it with one quick slash."

Kathy trusted Marcie's judgment. Marcie had learned to sew from her mother, and there was little about fabrics that she didn't know.

"Well, I guess Liz made me look like a fool again," said Kathy. "They're probably all still laughing."

"Not if Tom has anything to say about it," Marcie replied firmly. "He was really mad."

Mr. Price hung Kathy's coat in the hall closet and said, "Why don't you run upstairs and change?" He looked angry and disgusted, and Mrs. Price was close to tears.

Kathy walked up the stairs alone, listening to her mother offer to fix hot chocolate for them. Marcie's voice carried clearly. "I don't think I'm ever going to be able to eat again. Unless it's fried Liz Harper on toast."

"You'd be poisoned," Deb said. "I never thought I'd say this about anyone, but I think I hate her."

Kathy closed her bedroom door behind her. I won't cry, she promised herself. I won't give Liz the satisfaction.

She changed into jeans and a sweat shirt and hung the beautiful ruined dress in the closet. When she went back downstairs, she found a sober, quiet Tom in the living room.

"They were all gone when I got there," he told them. "Andy refused to play anymore, and the teachers sent everyone home."

"Lucky for Liz," Deb said.

"Andy was really mad, I heard. When I got there, some of the guys from the art department were just starting to clean up. They didn't know what had happened. I guess not everyone saw it. All they knew was that Andy said the band wasn't going to play anymore, and he told the teachers that he wasn't going to provide entertainment for a bunch of slobs. That's really what he said. He and the band walked out, so the teachers decided to cancel everything."

Marcie groaned. "All that work!" she cried. "It was all for nothing, just because Liz Harper thinks she can do anything she likes and get away with it."

"We could tell the school principal on Monday," Deb suggested.

Marcie shook her head. "He wouldn't believe it. As usual, no one who was in on it will admit it and none of us really saw her do it."

They sat in silence for several minutes, until Mr. Price said. "I think we're going to have to try to forget this ever happened. I wish I could tell you what we're supposed to learn from this experience, but frankly I don't know. I've heard of some mean things in my life, but this tops everything."

"I know what I learned," Deb replied. "To improve my taste in friends." She got up and hugged Kathy.

In a while, Deb, Marcie, and Tom left, after repeating how sorry they were. When the door closed behind them, Kathy told her parents that she was going to bed. "I think my cold is catching up with me. I don't feel very well, and it's not just because my dress was ruined and everyone in school got a chance to see what sort of panties I wear." She tried to laugh, but the laugh caught in her throat. "Good night," she said and went to her room.

Late that night, after her parents went to bed, Kathy lay awake, hugging a pillow to her chest. I'll live through this, she thought.

After all, in a hundred years, who'll know the difference?

But oh, I wish I had never met Liz Harper!

Chapter 13

Kathy's cold rapidly worsened, and on Monday her mother took her back to the doctor. He diagnosed her condition as bronchitis and ordered her to bed for several days. She would never have admitted it to anyone, but she was almost grateful for her illness. It kept her away from school and what she was certain would be days of ridicule until some other unlucky student provided the other students with something to laugh at. She stayed in her room, eating her meals in bed, and refused her mother's offer of the small TV the Prices kept in their bedroom.

Marcie and Deb called many times, but Kathy was too ill to go to the phone, so they dropped by the house and left books and flowers for her. Andy sent her joke greeting cards and a tape of their talent show act, but Kathy did not want to hear it, and the cassette lay on her desk, forgotten.

If she thought about anyone, it was Kevin. She wondered if he had heard about what had happened to her at the dance, and decided that there was no way he couldn't have found out. It was not a secret that could be kept. He probably wouldn't want anything to do with a girl who'd been publicly humiliated the way she had. He had dropped a note off at the house for her, but all it said was "Get well and come back soon."

Although she was out of school for two weeks, when she returned she expected to encounter remarks about her ruined dress and the dance; but strangely, no one said a word to her, although she felt she was being stared at every time she set foot in the halls.

On her first day back, Liz and Pris were both out with colds, and Kathy was grateful for their absence. It took all her strength simply to attend her classes; she had no energy left for confrontations.

Miss Correy, the trig teacher, was not sympathetic toward Kathy's illness, however, and she asked Kathy to stay after class. Without meeting Kathy's eyes, she told her that she was failing the class, and that unless her "attitude" changed immediately, she would receive a failing grade at the end of the semester. Kathy looked dully at Miss Correy while the woman spoke, and when she finished, Kathy walked away without answering. What was the use of trying to explain that her "attitude" had nothing to do with her long absence or with her problems in the class before that? Somewhere in her schooling, she had been badly prepared for trig, and the lack was showing now.

Marcie was waiting for her in the hall. "You look awful. What did old Stone Heart want with you this time?"

"She told me I'm failing, but that's not exactly a news flash," Kathy said. "I'm too tired to care."

"Why don't you go see your adviser? Maybe she can get through to Miss Correy."

Kathy shrugged. "I really don't care. I'm never going to love trig anyway, so what difference does it make?"

"None," Marcie said. "Don't worry about it. The only thing that matters now is that you're back in school." She stopped suddenly, and her face registered a new idea. "You could drop the class and take a study period! Lots of the kids do it. Maybe next semester trig will seem easier."

"I already thought of that," Kathy replied. "I think I will, but not today. I just want to finish out botany and choir, and then go home and crawl back in bed. I feel like my legs are made of spaghetti."

Marcie groaned. "Please don't mention food. Bibi cut off my cookie supply, and all I've got in our locker now is a jar of salad dressing she made today, with nothing to put it on."

"Put it in Miss Correy's mailbox in the office," Kathy suggested dispiritedly, and she headed toward her next class, leaving Marcie shouting with laughter in the hall behind her.

She saw Kevin for the first time in two weeks. He was in the greenhouse, talking with the botany teacher, and one of Liz's friends was standing next to him. When Kathy walked in, the girl saw her and walked away, but not before Kathy saw the smirk on her face. Then Kevin noticed her, and as soon as the teacher finished speaking to him, he hurried to Kathy. "I'm glad to see you back in school. You look great."

"No, I don't," Kathy said. "Believe me, I know what I look like."

"Did you get the note I left for you? Your mom said you weren't taking any phone calls."

Kathy nodded, and looked up at him tiredly. "I got the note, and thanks. I know how busy you are."

"Not too busy to remember a sick friend," he said. "Listen, I was wondering if you felt well enough to go downtown with me after school? There's something I want to show you."

Another time Kathy would have leapt at the chance, but on this day, she was too ill. "Sorry," she replied. "I don't feel that good yet. What was it that you wanted to show me?"

"Oh, I guess it's not that important. Maybe when you're up to it, you'll let me take you downtown for a surprise."

The teacher called the class to order then, and afterward, though Kevin walked her to choir, he didn't repeat his invitation.

She had seen Andy several times during the day, as she always did, but when she entered the choir room, she was unprepared for what he did.

"Okay, group, let's hear it!" he shouted as she walked in, and to her astonishment, the choir began to clap and call her name. Kevin was grinning, so she knew that he had been in on the surprise. When the racket finally died down, Mr. King welcomed Kathy back with a rambling speech, and at long last she was allowed to take her seat. "I hope," Mr. King said, "that your voice hasn't changed."

Kathy shook her head, embarrassed. "I'm just a little hoarse, that's all."

"Good," he said. "Because today we're beginning rehearsals for the Christmas program, and I've got some work cut out for you."

It was good to be back, she thought. She saw Kevin, still smiling at her, and she smiled back weakly.

The next time he invited her to go downtown, she'd go, she thought. No matter what, she'd go.

She was late getting to her locker after choir, but Marcie was not in sight, so Kathy leaned against the wall and waited while the other students got their coats, books, and umbrellas, and left. Outside, rain was blowing against the building, and the last of the autumn leaves were heaped in soggy piles on the street. Kathy was in no hurry to go out in the storm, so she did not mind waiting.

When Marcie finally appeared, she looked guilty. "Thanks for waiting," she said. "I wasn't sure you would, but I couldn't come out of the john before this. I didn't want anyone to see me." She held up a large paper sack. "Five jars of that awful salad dressing the home ec class made this morning. Bibi's makes six. Everyone was glad to donate to the cause."

"What cause?" Kathy asked bewilderedly. "I don't think I like salad dressing enough to want six jars of it."

"It's not for you, dummy!" Marcie said. "I wouldn't give this awful junk to anyone I liked. It's for Liz!"

"What? She wasn't even here today, and if she had been, she would have left a long time ago. Anyway, since when do you give her presents?"

"Since today. Bibi and I decided that we should be more generous. Now watch this."

Marcie dug through her purse until she came up with a plastic funnel, which she inserted into the ventilation panel on Liz's locker, opposite where the top shelf would be. Then she began pouring the first jar of salad dressing into the funnel.

"I don't think you'd better do that!" Kathy warned. "She'll be furious."

"Good! I've wanted to do something to her for a long time, but Mom made me promise that I wouldn't punch her lights out. It has something to do with being a lady, I think."

Marcie replaced the first jar, now empty, in the sack and took out another. The thin dressing poured easily and now the hall smelled of garlic. "She's going to kill you," Kathy predicted.

"She's not going to know who did it. We all took a solemn oath." Marcie was pouring the third jar now.

Two boys came down the hall, and Marcie quickly pulled out the funnel and stood before Liz's locker innocently.

"You ought to change your perfume, Marcie," one of them said, and the other one laughed.

"It isn't me!" Marcie cried. "I don't know what smells so awful."

She waited until the boys turned the corner and were out of sight before she put the funnel back in the ventilation panel. It took only minutes for her to empty the last of the jars, and by that time a small trickle of dressing was working its way out from under the locker door.

"The custodian will see that and he'll clean up the mess," Kathy said.

"You must think I was born yesterday," Marcie complained. "The custodian left for Seattle an hour ago to pick up his wife at the airport, and his assistant has too much other work to do this afternoon. He won't be able to inspect the halls today."

"How do you know?" Kathy asked suspiciously.

Marcie turned angelic eyes on her. "I am not responsible for the broken pipe in the boy's john on the third floor," she explained. "But," she continued, beginning to laugh, "I believe in taking advantage of opportunity, and what better opportunity could I have than Mr. Johnson going off to the airport and the antique plumbing giving way upstairs?"

"Let's get out of here," Kathy said. "I think we've been lucky so far, but I have a hunch that the long arm of judgment is about to grab both of us."

As they left the building, Marcie said, "Just remember one thing. You had nothing to do with this. Absolutely nothing. But Bibi and I thought you deserved to watch. Andy knows, too. He's the one who told me about the flood upstairs."

Kathy shook her head wonderingly. "You never stop surprising me," she said. "You're the last person I would have expected to pull off a stunt like that."

Marcie shrugged, tipping her umbrella, and a cascade of rain fell on her. "Everyone has her limits. Let's say that Liz reached mine about fifteen years ago."

"But you're only sixteen!"

"So? She threw sand at me in the playground sandbox." Marcie giggled.

"You've got an answer for everything," said Kathy. "I just hope you've got one when someone accuses you of the great garlic caper."

That night she and her parents discussed her problems in trig, and all were in agreement that it would be best if Kathy dropped the class. She was relieved that they understood and sympathized with her.

Her father told her that she should be careful not to blame herself. "It's only one class," he said. "And you tried your best. We know what a good student you are."

Marcie said almost the same thing the next morning, so Kathy went to the office feeling confident, rather than burning with shame, and she told her adviser what she wanted. By the time the bell rang for first period, the necessary forms had been filled out, and Kathy walked to her locker with a light heart.

There was a small riot going on in the hall. Students milled about, laughing, ignoring the first bell, and several teachers were demanding quiet and order and getting neither. Kathy pushed her way through the crowd until she reached her locker, which she found standing open. Pris stood nearby, with another of Liz's friends, and neither of them saw Kathy while she hung up her coat.

Across the hall Liz was shouting, "I want to know who

did this! I want to know right now!"

The air was thick with garlic fumes, and Kathy, without being able to see through the crowd, knew that Liz had opened her locker.

Marcie squeezed past Pris and said loudly, "Guess what, Kathy? Someone poured something all over Liz's books. It smells like garlic. And no one knows how the stuff got in there, either. Someone must have a key to her locker."

Pris studied Marcie's face and then Kathy's, looking for signs of laughter. "You two don't care," she hissed angrily. "Her books are probably ruined, and she left a very expensive scarf on the shelf, too."

"Aren't you glad you don't share a locker with her, then," Kathy replied. "Your books would have been ruined." She was reminding Pris of her insistence on having the locker shelf all to herself, and the barb was not lost on the homely girl.

Pris turned away angrily, and Marcie covered her mouth with her hands to hide her laughter.

"Don't say one word," Kathy whispered. "Don't laugh, either."

They made their way through the crowd just as the final bell rang, and both broke into a run. They were late to their first-period classes, but Marcie obviously thought the tardy slip would be worth it. Kathy wasn't so sure. She was afraid her friend would be caught, because too many people knew where the salad dressing had come from.

But at lunchtime Marcie was still laughing, and while she, Deb, and Kathy waited in line for lunch, she whispered avidly, filling them in on the details of Liz's adventures with the garlic dressing.

"It came off the covers of her books, darn it," she told them, "but her scarf will never be the same. And even after they scrubbed out her locker with disinfectant, it still reeks of garlic. The custodian had to assign her a new locker. The whole hall smells like garlic. I think it killed the flies all the way to the kitchen."

Deb made a face. "You may be able to eat after saying something disgusting like that, but no one else can. Why don't you get sick when you're telling an awful story like that?"

"I'm immune because of all *your* awful stories, that's why," Marcie retorted. "Listen, you didn't let me tell the best part. Liz smells like garlic, too. Honestly, you can't get near her without your eyes watering."

Kathy watched Deb's face, worried that she might feel some resentment toward Marcie for the trick she had played on Liz, but Deb was smiling. Kathy ate her lunch quickly, although she had little appetite. She was worried about Marcie, and Bibi, too, but they didn't seem concerned about being caught.

Instead of going to trig after lunch, Kathy went to the study hall on the south side of the building, where the tall windows looked out over bare trees lightly silvered with frost. Winter was coming to Port Borden, and spring seemed a million years away.

Kathy was shown to a seat in the row next to the windows, and, to her astonishment, the student sitting directly in front of her was Kevin. He looked up and smiled when she passed him, then bent his head over a book. Kathy tried to concentrate on her history homework, but found the task impossible. She caught herself staring at Kevin's back. He was wearing the fisherman's sweater again, and by the time the period was over she knew the pattern of the knit well enough to have made the sweater herself, she thought.

The bell rang and Kevin swung around in his seat, facing her. "How are you feeling today?"

"Lots better. I dropped trig, so that's why I'm in here."

"Most of the kids here are seniors who have already taken nearly all of their required subjects. I ended up with two study periods, which works out great. I hardly ever have any homework to do after I leave school."

He stood up and picked up her books as well as his own. "Come on. I'll walk you to botany."

Kathy followed him up the aisle, conscious of the eyes watching her. How many of them are thinking about the dance? she wondered. She lifted her chin a little higher.

"Can you come downtown with me this afternoon?"

Kathy blinked in surprise. "Why, sure, I guess so. Does this have something to do with what you wanted to show me?"

"Yes," he replied. "You seemed interested in my hobby, so I wanted you to see something I made."

"What is it?"

"Wait and see," he said. "I'll meet you in the school parking lot right after choir. Okay?"

Kathy nodded, mystified and pleased. Whatever he wanted to show her must be special. Just as they parted to go to their separate tables in botany, Kevin reached out and touched her hand briefly, sending an electric thrill up her arm. She knew she was blushing, but she didn't care.

Marcie was right about Liz. She did smell of garlic, and several of the students commented on it. Liz's famous temper flared and she stormed out of the class. She had not returned by the end of the period, and she was not in choir, either. Kathy decided that Liz had probably gone home, and she couldn't blame her.

When Kathy met Marcie at their lockers after choir, she told her friend that Kevin had asked her to go downtown with him, so she would not be walking home with Marcie.

"I wish you could see the way he looks at you when you aren't watching," Marcie said.

Kathy shook her head. "You imagine things." But she was happy as she left the building, and she hoped that the garlic smell had not saturated her winter coat. It seemed to linger everywhere, a reminder of Liz.

Kevin was waiting by his car, and she hurried to join him. "Now tell me what this is all about," she demanded.

He refused, grinning, and since she was enjoying the suspense as much as he was, she didn't ask him again to tell her why he wanted her with him. He drove past his father's pharmacy and parked near a small jewelry store. Quickly, he got out of the car, opened Kathy's door, and took her arm, leading her to the jewelry store window.

"Look," he said, pointing to a small silver charm displayed there.

Kathy leaned close to the window and studied the charm.

It was a small square, and carved on it was a rosebud, perfect in every way. The design was so intricate that she marveled over it. "You made this?" she asked. "It's beautiful!"

"Mr. Hansen, the man who owns the store, said he'd take it on consignment. I'm hoping that someone buys it before Christmas. The profit I make will be my Christmas spending money."

Inside the store, a small, elderly man looked up and saw them standing outside. He gestured for them to enter, and Kevin took Kathy's hand as they walked in.

He introduced Kathy to Mr. Hansen, explaining to the man that he had wanted Kathy to see the charm. Mr. Hansen was pleased, and he took the charm from the window so that Kathy could see it better.

"Kevin is very talented," he said. "It's too bad that most silver jewelry is made on a production line these days. There aren't many real silversmiths left."

Kathy turned the charm over, and on the back she saw a tiny KW engraved on one corner, so small that if she had not been examining the charm closely, she would never have seen it.

She looked up at Kevin. "It's the most beautiful charm I ever saw. I'm sure someone will buy it."

Mr. Hansen nodded eagerly. "No doubt about it," he agreed. "And I'm willing to display Kevin's work here any time he wants me to. I'm proud to put jewelry like this in my window."

Kathy gave the charm back to the man, and she and Kevin left the shop. "Your folks must be excited," she said.

"Sure. Everyone is happy but Peggy. She wanted the charm for her bracelet." He laughed then, as he walked her to his car. "What she doesn't know is that I'm making her one just like it for Christmas."

"That's nice of you. She'll be surprised, I bet."

"If I can keep it hidden from her."

When they were in his car, he said, "I wish I didn't have to take you home so soon, but I have to be at work in a few minutes."

"I know," replied Kathy. "And I have a mountain of homework to catch up on. But I'm glad you showed me the charm. I know the next time I'm down here, it will be gone. Someone will buy it."

When he stopped the car in front of the Price house, he turned to face her, and his crooked grin seemed to light up his whole face. "Thanks again for coming with me. I won't forget that you were the first one after my family to know the charm was there." He touched her hand once more, briefly.

Mrs. Price had been watching from the living room window, and when Kathy went in the house, she asked, "Who was that gorgeous person?"

"Oh, that's just Kevin," Kathy said. "His dad owns the drugstore. He gave me a ride home."

She couldn't share her feelings with her mother yet. Later, when she was accustomed to the idea that Kevin had singled her out, she would tell her folks and Marcie and Deb about the charm. But for the time being, she wanted to keep that half an hour of her life a secret.

As she walked up the stairs to her room, her mother lifted her eyebrows. "Just a ride?" she said to a houseplant.

"What?" Kathy called down. "Were you talking to me?"

"No, I was talking to something still living on this planet," Mrs. Price replied, laughing, and she went back to the couch and picked up her book.

Chapter 14

Kevin's silver charm was gone from the window on the following Saturday when Kathy went past the jewelry store, and she smiled in satisfaction. She was with Marcie and Deb, and she had told them about the charm, so they were disappointed that they had not seen it. When Mr. Hansen saw her standing outside the store, he waved, and Kathy grinned in return.

"It must be nice having a boyfriend who has a better hobby than tinkering forever with his car," Marcie said.

"Hey, look out," Kathy warned. "My mother's hobby is tinkering with the car." The girls laughed then. Mrs. Price's strange hobby amused everyone, but several people had taken advantage of it. Mrs. Price had fixed Marcie's bike, taught Deb how to change the oil in her little car, and she had come to Tom's rescue on more than one occasion.

The girls turned into the largest department store in Port Borden, exclaiming over the Christmas decorations.

"I love Christmas, but why does it have to come so fast? Halloween is hardly over, and it's time to start making Christmas lists," Marcie said.

Deb glanced at the list in her hand. "You had to say it, didn't you. I'll bet your list is complete and you know everything you're going to give everyone. Please don't tell me about it and ruin my day."

Marcie tapped her forehead. "My list is all right here.

I'm giving everyone a gingerbread man and a pound of peanut brittle."

"I believe you," answered Deb. "I wish I didn't, but I actually believe that you'd do something like that."

"Sounds good to me," Kathy said.

"Well, there's one exception," admitted Marcie. "I'm giving Liz a clove of garlic."

The three girls burst out laughing. Marcie had escaped detection, and the mystery of who put the garlic salad dressing in Liz's locker had never been solved. Kathy never walked past Liz's locker without thinking about it and marveling again that Marcie would do something so outrageous. It only proved, she decided, that there was a limit to the frustration anyone could take. But at least Marcie didn't make herself sick over things.

But then, neither did Deb, and she didn't relieve the pressures she felt about things in such a wild, silly way. Deb always just shrugged and kept on going. Would she ever find her own way of coping with Liz? Kathy wondered.

It was dark by the time Deb dropped Kathy off at her house. The Prices had put up their Christmas tree early because it had been so many years since they had been able to celebrate the holiday together in their own home, and as Kathy walked up her front steps, she admired the colored lights she saw through the window. They had gotten the biggest tree Mr. Price could fit in the high-ceilinged room, and Kathy stood outside the window for several minutes, enjoying it. When she went in and found that both her parents were in the kitchen, she quickly ran upstairs to hide the presents she had bought in the back of her closet. When she came back downstairs, she had changed into an old pair of wool slacks and a heavy sweater, and her cheeks were still pink from the cold outside.

"Kevin called you," her father said. He smiled briefly at her, then turned his attention to the steaming cup of coffee on the table in front of him.

Kathy's heart jumped. Kevin had never called her before,

even though they spoke together often each day. "Did he leave a message?"

"No. He just said he'd call back. He seems like a nice young man."

Kathy tried to shrug indifferently and failed to carry it off. "He really is nice!" she blurted.

"And I'll bet he wears a watch, so he's on time, too," her father said, reminding her of Gordon's failure to arrive the night he was to take her to a movie.

Kathy smiled, but a circle of ice chilled her heart. "I hope so," she replied. Her father had never forgiven Gordon for his bad manners, even though Kathy seldom thought about the incident anymore. Gordon had never said more than "Hi" to her since that night, but he had never looked the least bit apologetic, either. Well, she thought, what did it matter? She didn't like him anyway, and he was still going steady with Liz, even though Liz's idea of going steady certainly seemed different from anyone else's.

Liz flirted constantly with any boy who attracted her attention, and didn't seem to care if it bothered Gordon. Oh, who cares? Kathy thought impatiently. They aren't a part of my life.

What mattered was that Kevin had called her and would call her back, and who knew what he might ask? Perhaps he had a night off from his work at the pharmacy and wanted her to go to a movie with him. Anything was possible.

Promptly at six o'clock, the phone rang, and Kathy answered it. Kevin recognized her voice, although many people mistook her for her mother, and he asked her immediately if she liked to ice-skate.

"I love it!" she exclaimed. "We used to skate every weekend at St. Catherine's."

"Then would you like to go skating tomorrow afternoon? I don't have to work then, and we could go to the ice rink right after lunch and stay the whole afternoon."

"I'd like that very much," she said. She couldn't believe that this was finally happening.

"Would you like to have lunch with me, too?" he asked.

This was too much. "Lunch?" asked Kathy, as if she had never heard the word before. "Really?"

Kevin's laugh was soft. "We could go to that place where we had hamburgers that time, or we could eat at the snack bar in the ice rink. Which would you like?"

She could not have decided if her life depended on it. "You choose," she said.

"Then I think we should go back to that place where we went before. I liked the food there, but it means a bit of a drive. Is that all right with you?"

"It's wonderful!" cried Kathy. "What time shall I be ready?"

"Twelve-thirty," he replied. "I'll see you then."

She was reluctant to let him hang up. She felt as if she could guarantee that he was real if she could keep him on the line a little longer, but something told her that it would be a mistake to hang on to him, even over the phone, so she thanked him again and put down the receiver.

She rushed into the kitchen, her eyes as bright as a child's on Christmas morning. "He asked me to go ice-skating!" she told them. "And we're having lunch, too."

"Hmm," her father said. "It seems to me that your mother and I used to go skating, once upon a time. Do you suppose that Kevin would mind if we came along?"

"Daddy!" Kathy cried, alarmed.

"He's only joking," Mrs. Price said firmly. "Don't let him tease you."

"Who said I was teasing?" Mr. Price demanded. But Kathy saw the smile he was trying to hide, so she bent down and hugged him. "You can't fool me, Dad."

She danced out of the room, too excited even to think about anything else. Tomorrow! she thought exultantly. Tomorrow! She didn't know if she could bear to wait that long.

That evening, it took her half an hour to find her skates, which had been packed away in a box and stored in the basement with dozens of other boxes. Her skating clothes were hanging in the storage closet, and she knew they would still fit. Her grandmother had made the short, bright-red velvet skirt, and the red sweater had been a present from her parents. She herself had knitted the white cap and scarf, decorating both with red tassels. She knew how pretty she looked in the outfit, and she was a very good skater. Everything would be absolutely perfect, she was sure.

Light snow fell during the night, and Port Borden was a magic place the next day. By noon the clouds were gone, but the snow remained, glittering under a bright sun, and every branch on every tree was coated with a thin film of ice.

At noon, Kathy dressed in her skating costume, and she pulled a heavy, dark-blue skirt over the short red one, because they were having lunch at a restaurant before skating. Promptly at twelve-thirty, Kevin knocked at the front door and Mr. Price let him in. Kathy introduced Kevin to her mother and picked up her skates. Her mother winked at her solemnly, when Kevin and her dad were examining his skates, and Kathy winked back with more confidence than she felt.

"We'll be back around six," Kevin told her parents, and they walked out the door together.

"I'm really hungry," he said as they drove away. "I hope you are, too."

"Starved," she replied, although food had not crossed her mind until that moment.

They ate quickly, because both of them were anxious to skate, and Kathy was surprised how easy it was to talk to Kevin. The nervousness she had felt before when talking to him had disappeared. He was bright and funny, laughing as easily as Andy, but always there was a serious undertone to everything he said, as though he were older than the other students at the high school. Kathy found his maturity very attractive.

Sunday was family day at the ice rink, and when they arrived there were already several small children stumbling around the ice, guided by patient parents. One older couple, dressed alike in bulky gray sweaters and dark-gray slacks, skated hand in hand like teenagers, and Kevin and Kathy exchanged a quick, delighted smile.

It took them only moments to lace up their skates and for Kathy to slip off the heavy blue skirt, and then Kevin led her out onto the ice. He was a wonderful skater, every bit as experienced as she was, and they skated together comfortably, as if they had done it many times before. Once he led her to the center of the rink and took both her hands, then spun her around at arm's length until she was dizzy. When he finally let her stop, the other people at the rink applauded, and the older couple tried the same thing, only not so fast. Several children attempted to imitate them, also, and they stumbled and fell, laughing wildly. Time sped by, and the first break came at three-thirty, when most of the families left, taking the tired children home. Kevin bought tickets for the next session, and Kathy waited for him on a bench, drinking the coffee he had brought her before he'd left. She had never liked coffee before, but on that day she would cheerfully have tried anything Kevin offered.

Teenagers came in now, many of them skillful skaters, and Kathy saw several students from Port Borden High there. She and Kevin were greeted enthusiastically by their fellow students, and Kathy was told by one girl that this group met every Sunday. "We're sort of a club, but not exactly," the girl, Sherry, explained. "We've done this every winter since grade school."

"Sounds like fun," Kathy replied wistfully, and Kevin overheard her.

"We'll have to come back soon, won't we?" he said. "If you'd like to, that is."

She nodded, too pleased to speak, and he led her out onto the ice again, this time to waltz with her in perfect time to the recorded music.

"You're a good skater," he told her when the waltz was over. "You're as good as my sister, and she's the one who taught me."

"You mean Peggy?" Kathy asked impishly, knowing that Peggy was only a little girl.

"Sure." Kevin laughed. "Peggy still skates on her bottom. But we have hopes for her."

"We could bring her with us next time," Kathy said slyly.

"Not on your life!" Kevin exclaimed. "I don't want to share you with that spoiled brat." He spun Kathy around breathlessly for a moment and then pulled her beside him.

"If she's such a brat, how come you're working so hard on that silver charm for her Christmas present?" Kathy asked.

"You remembered that? Well, she can be cute sometimes. I sold that other charm, the one I left in Mr. Hansen's window."

"I know. I saw that it was gone. Are you going to make something else to put there?"

"Yes, I've already started it. But I won't say what it is until I've finished. Then I'll take you down and show it to you."

He was including Kathy in many of his plans, and she was thrilled about this new turn of events. It was as if he were taking for granted that she would be a part of his life for the rest of his senior year, and this made all sorts of things possible.

Contented, she skated with his arm around her until she was exhausted, and when the rink closed at five-thirty, she was ready to unlace her skates and leave. "I'm so tired, I don't think I'll be able to walk tomorrow," she said.

"You must need more practice," he replied, looking down at her and smiling his delicious, crooked smile. "We'll see what we can do about that."

But he didn't name a day they would go skating again. And, while Kathy waited all the way home for him to say something definite, he never did.

At her front door, she asked him if he would like to come in the house for a while, but he refused, saying that he was expected for dinner at his house. Disappointed, Kathy began to turn away, one hand on the doorknob, when Kevin put both his hands on her shoulders and turned her back to face him. Under the porch light his amber eyes looked dark, and he wasn't smiling. Suddenly, without warning, he bent and kissed her lightly on her lips, and then let go of her shoulders.

"Thanks for coming with me," he said softly. He left

her, and ran down the steps, taking them two at a time.

Dazed, Kathy turned and went inside. He kissed me, she thought numbly, and she brushed her fingers over her lips.

"Did you have a good time?" her father asked her from the dining room door.

"Oh, sure," she said casually. "It was nice."

But then she ran up the stairs quickly, before he could see the expression on her face.

Another secret to keep! Kevin had kissed her.

Chapter 15

Kevin did not take her skating again until the week after Christmas, but she knew he was thinking about her, because on the night of the high school Christmas program, he told her that he would have liked to spend another Sunday afternoon with her, but that his family kept him busy on Sundays during the holiday season. "I have more aunts and uncles and cousins than anyone else I know, and they all like to get together over Christmas."

Kathy understood and envied him. She had few relatives herself, and the Prices would be spending Christmas alone, just the three of them.

Marcie invited Kathy and Deb to spend the night with her three days before Christmas, and the girls had a small, private party of their own. They exchanged presents, stuffed themselves with candy and Christmas cookies, which had been provided by Deb's mother who was famous for her party treats, and sat up most of the night watching Christmas programs on television. When they parted the next morning, they were all sleepy, and Kathy went home for a nap, grateful that they were on Christmas vacation and she had no homework to worry about.

She did not wake up until late in the afternoon, just as her mother was returning from her last-minute Christmas shopping. Kathy joined her mother in the kitchen and fixed herself a cup of strong tea.

"Pajama parties are fun, but it takes a while to recover," she admitted ruefully.

"I remember," her mother replied. She sat down at the table with Kathy. "Do you know a red-haired girl, very pretty, about your age?"

"That sounds like Liz," said Kathy. "Was it the same red-haired girl you saw in choir at the music festival?"

Mrs. Price pulled her gloves off slowly as she thought. "I don't remember. All I was noticing that night was you. This girl has hair a little longer than shoulder-length, and not too curly. She's very attractive."

"That's probably Liz," Kathy said. "Why?"

"I saw her in the drugstore when I stopped by for that hand lotion you like, and by the way, it's in the sack in the hall."

Liz was in the drugstore? Well, why not? That didn't mean she was there to see Kevin, and maybe he wasn't even working today. Unwillingly, Kathy asked, "What was she doing?"

"She and a friend of hers were talking to Kevin," answered Mrs. Price. "The other girl is rather thin, and not nearly as attractive as Liz."

"Probably Pris Burke," Kathy offered dispiritedly. "I'm not crazy about either one of them."

Mrs. Price was silent then, and Kathy wondered what she was holding back. She knew her mother well enough to know that she wouldn't volunteer bad news. "Was Liz flirting with Kevin?" Kathy asked.

Mrs. Price considered this for a moment. "I'd say she was, yes."

"She does that all the time," Kathy told her in disgust. "She's going steady with Gordon, but she flirts with every boy in school, especially Kevin."

The question she did not dare ask must have been written on her face, because her mother said, "Well, he didn't seem too impressed."

"I hope it stays that way," replied Kathy. She drank her tea and let the conversation drop.

Maybe I should send him a Christmas card, she thought, but again she decided against it. She did not feel comfortable making gestures that might not be returned, and she certainly did not want to obligate Kevin to her in any way. She had received no holiday greeting from any boy except the irrepressible Andy, who had sent her an outrageous picture of himself in a Santa Claus suit with clown makeup on his face.

She had shown the picture to Marcie, but Marcie had received one, too. "I'd sleep with it under my pillow, but he doesn't deserve such a romantic gesture," Marcie had said irritably, and Kathy had laughed in spite of herself. Marcie's secret fantasy about Andy still remained a secret between them, and Kathy never ceased to wonder at Andy's blindness toward her friend. Someday, she thought, she was going to drop Andy a big hint.

Christmas passed happily at the Price house, with all three of them enjoying the holiday together and in their own home at last, and when Kevin called Kathy the day after Christmas, it was an added treat. He wanted to go ice-skating with her again, he told her. All his relatives had gone back home again, and he had his Sundays free.

This time they ate at the snack bar at the ice rink, although the food was terrible. They laughed together at the small, soggy hamburgers and thin shakes.

"Let's not do this part of it again," Kevin said. "Not even Marcie would have enjoyed this hamburger."

"Have you heard about her appetite, too?" Kathy asked.

"Sure." Kevin laughed. "Once Andy said he'd ask her out for dinner, but he isn't old enough to get a bank loan."

Kathy laughed in spite of herself. "That's really mean of him. He can say the most horrible things about people."

"He doesn't mean any harm, though," Kevin said. "I think it's just part of his act. He has a great sense of humor."

"Sure, as long as you don't care about him one way or the other," replied Kathy. "Except as a friend, I mean. But if someone did care about him, he sure could make that someone miserable." She was thinking aloud, remembering Marcie's unhappiness.

She found Kevin looking at her strangely. "I didn't know you felt that way about him," he said quietly. "You told me you were only friends."

"I wasn't talking about me!" Kathy blurted. "I was talking about Marcie!"

Oh, no! She had babbled Marcie's secret! Kevin was staring at her, confused. "Marcie! You mean Marcie likes Andy? It's not you?"

"Of course it's not me!" Kathy stormed. "And I never should have said anything about Marcie. She'll never forgive me if she finds out. Promise you won't repeat what I said to anyone, especially Andy."

Kevin nodded. "Sure, I promise. I'm really surprised, though."

Kathy finished her shake before she spoke again. "I know. You thought it was me. Well, you were wrong. Now I think we'd better drop the subject. I feel bad enough as it is."

"Consider it dropped for all time," Kevin said. "Come on, let's skate. We'll go somewhere else and eat later on."

Kathy whirled out onto the ice with him, glad to feel his arm around her again, and immediately forgot their conversation about Marcie and Andy. But later, when they had gone to their favorite restaurant again to make up for the disappointing lunch, Kevin brought up Andy once more.

"I used to think that Andy and you were more than just friends," he admitted. "You were always together, and you seemed to be having such a good time. It was only after the talent show that I saw you weren't spending much time with him anymore, and that's when I decided that it would be all right to ask you out myself."

Kathy looked up at him, ignoring the hamburger on her plate. "I don't know how you could have thought that," she replied. "We went to the ball together, but it was only as friends."

"Yeah, I heard about that," Kevin said briefly, and Kathy's eyes fell.

I'll bet you did, she thought. "Well," she went on firmly, "I still don't know how you got the idea Andy and I were going together. He takes out a sophomore. I don't even remember her name."

"Sandy," Kevin supplied, and Kathy burst out laughing.

"Gee," she said. "You're really up on things."

"Not everything," he replied seriously. "Only those things that have to do with you. Liz was the one who told me you and Andy were serious about each other. She said you just had some things to work out, that's all. I wasn't sure whether or not to believe her."

Kathy was outraged. "Liz doesn't know anything about me, and Andy can't stand her, so he'd never confide in her."

Kevin leaned back in his chair, his face impassive, and Kathy wondered what he was thinking. "Andy's a good guy," he said finally. "I never could see why you'd be interested in Gordon. He doesn't treat Liz very well."

"That's what she told you?" Kathy asked, astonished.

Kevin shrugged. "It's pretty obvious."

The only thing obvious to Kathy was that Liz flirted with everyone, no matter what Gordon thought, and although Kathy didn't like Gordon, she almost felt sorry for him. But there was no point in arguing the issue with Kevin, for he had made up his mind to sympathize with Liz.

Kathy changed the subject abruptly and asked Kevin about his hobby. "When will you have more of your jewelry in Mr. Hansen's window?" she asked. "Every time I pass the store, I hope to see something of yours there."

"In a few more weeks," Kevin replied. "I have a lot of work to do on the piece yet, but it's coming along better than I expected."

"And you're not going to tell me what it is," Kathy said. She was smiling, knowing his answer in advance.

"And I'm not going to tell you," he agreed easily. "I like to surprise people."

I should say you do, she thought. One moment she felt secure in his affection and the next moment she wondered exactly what he did think of her. It was, she thought, an uncomfortable position to be in.

That afternoon he took her home earlier than he had the last time they went skating. The wintery daylight was just beginning to fade.

"I had a wonderful time," she told him.

"Good. So did I." He took her hand as they went up her

steps. "See you tomorrow in study hall," he said, and he smiled as she went in the door.

I wish it had been dark, she thought as she closed the door behind her. Maybe he would have kissed me again.

Maybe next time.

But two weeks later, when he invited her to go skating again, he told her that Deb and Tom would be going with them. Although she had a wonderful time, there was no opportunity for them to talk alone except while they were skating, and when he took her home, Deb and Tom were still in the car. She told Marcie afterward that hers had to be the quietest romance on record, and Marcie agreed that she was probably right, with one exception.

"I was alone with Andy for half an hour one afternoon," Marcie said disgustedly. "He spent the whole time talking about the new strings he had put on his guitar."

"Now that's romance," replied Kathy, and she burst out laughing.

In March, when the last of the winter frosts was over and the first buds were appearing on the trees, Kevin asked Kathy to accompany him downtown after school, and she knew without asking that he was going to show her the jewelry he had been working on all winter long.

This time when he led her up to the store window, he pointed to the center piece in the display and Kathy gasped. There, on a piece of blue silk, was a beautiful silver necklace made of dozens of small silver leaves dangling from a thin silver chain. The leaves were so perfectly created that the veins showed on each one, and the edges of each leaf were delicately notched.

"Oh, Kevin!" she cried. "I never saw anything like it. Someone will buy it before the week is over."

"I don't know about that," he replied doubtfully. "It's pretty expensive. Mr. Hansen wasn't sure how soon it would sell."

"You just wait," she said confidently.

Mr. Hansen saw them outside together and waved to them, even though he was waiting on a customer at the time. Although his store was small, he was usually busy.

"What are you going to do with all the money you'll get?" Kathy asked.

"You're looking at part of my tuition for my first quarter at the university," he told her.

"Really?" Kathy was impressed. "Is that how you plan on putting yourself through school?"

"That, with what I've been earning working for my dad. I'll be staying in a dormitory, so that costs a lot, too. But I'm sure I'll be able to do it."

"Dormitories aren't much fun," Kathy said. "I had enough of them when I was in boarding school."

"Then where are you planning to stay when you go to college? It's too far to commute, even if you go to the University of Washington."

Kathy stuck her hands in her pockets to warm them. The wind that blew across the Sound apparently didn't know that spring was almost there. "I don't even know what I want to do yet. Dad keeps asking me, and so far I haven't been able to make up my mind."

Since Kevin had another hour before he had to go to work that day, they walked slowly along the sidewalk. "You said once you liked botany," he reminded her.

"Sure, but I'm not ready to commit myself yet." The conversation was making her sad. Next year Kevin would no longer be living in Port Borden. He'd be in college, and she'd only be a senior in high school.

How often would they see each other then?

Chapter 16

When spring came, the daffodils that Kathy had planted in the botany greenhouse were already in full bloom, and soon the ones she had planted at home opened out. Now the students were transplanting seedlings from the greenhouse to the school grounds, where flower beds circled many of the old trees. Kathy loved the work so much that her parents let her do anything she wished with the garden at home. Excitedly, she planted both flowers and vegetables in the backyard and spent much of her free time there. She felt creative as she worked among her young plants, and her hobby filled her with satisfaction.

Each Saturday she walked downtown to look at Kevin's necklace in the jewelry store window. He had been right. The necklace was slow to sell, and she knew he was concerned, so she tried to be encouraging.

Two events were circled on her calendar in April. The choir was performing in the spring music concert on the third Saturday of the month, and on the last Saturday there was to be another dance. This one, Marcie explained to Kathy, would be a Sadie Hawkins, giving the girls a chance to do the inviting.

"For once, we'll all have dates," Marcie said. "Well, almost everyone. There are always some girls who are too scared to ask a boy to go."

They were sitting in the cafeteria, and Deb was finishing her second piece of cake. "I already asked Tom," she told them smugly. "He said yes."

"It's your funeral," replied Marcie. "I wouldn't take my brother across the street."

"You don't appreciate his fine points," Deb said.

"You don't have to take his shoes off the coffee table every night!"

Kathy finished her milk and stacked her plates. "Who are you going to ask, Marcie?"

"You tell me first who you're asking," Marcie responded.

Kathy blushed and laughed. "I haven't made up my mind whether or not to go. If I ask Kevin he might say no. He'd have to take two Saturday nights off in a row, and maybe he won't want to do that. And don't you dare say that I won't find out unless I ask."

"That's exactly what I'm going to say." Marcie scraped her plate industriously.

"So if it's that easy, who are you going to ask?" Kathy demanded.

"Jim Abbott. He'll say yes to anything, as long as he doesn't have to pay for it."

"Gee, Marcie, that sounds really romantic," Deb said sarcastically.

"Who's talking about romance? I'm being practical. Mom is already making me a new dress, and if I want to wear it, I have to ask him to the dance. It's that simple."

"You could ask Gordon," Deb suggested. "He and Liz broke up again." She looked at Marcie to catch her reaction, and Kathy held her breath.

Marcie's face flamed. "I know. I heard," she said.

"Maybe if you tied an alarm clock around his neck, he'd be on time," Deb continued. "Or maybe the rest of us can gang up on him and convince him that he needs a watch."

Marcie shook her head slowly. "I don't think I'm interested."

"I know," said Deb. "It's because of what he did to Kathy. He really is a creep."

But that was not the whole problem, and Kathy knew it. For a long time Marcie had been telling people she liked Gordon because he was safely interested in someone else. As long as everyone thought she had a crush on Gordon, no one would suspect that she really cared about Andy. Kathy did not know of a solution to the problem. If Gordon was free again, Marcie was in a difficult position. Even Gordon thought that she was interested in him.

"Has the dance committee decided on a band yet?" she asked casually, wondering if Andy's group was already committed.

"They're hiring a group from Seattle," Deb said complacently, never knowing that she had probably just caused Marcie's heart to stop.

"Not Andy's group?" Kathy asked, wanting to be certain.

Deb shook her head. "No. He didn't ask for the job, or I'm sure he would have gotten it. I heard that two of the guys in the group are quitting, anyway. Both of them have to get steady jobs so they can save money for college next fall. The only ones left are juniors."

Kathy saw that Marcie's face was white. She really looked scared! Kathy could hardly believe it.

"I'm going to my locker," Kathy told them suddenly. "I forgot one of my books." She hurried away, knowing that Andy would be in the student activity center, as always, with the other drama club students. They were always rehearsing something.

Sure enough, he was deep in conversation with two other students when she found him, and it was difficult to pull him away. "I have to talk to you," she insisted.

"Who am I to deny you anything you want, prep school?" he replied. "What's your problem?"

"I want to talk to you about Marcie," she said. "Right now."

"Is she okay? Did she eat her plate for lunch by mistake?"

"I'm not going to laugh because that wasn't funny. Did you ever try to see how much you hurt her feelings when you make remarks like that?" Kathy's gray eyes flashed.

"Hey!" Andy yelled. "What did I do? You're coming down pretty hard on me, without telling me why."

"Stop teasing Marcie!" Kathy demanded. "Don't say one more mean thing to her. Is that clear enough?"

Andy looked appalled. "What mean thing did I ever say? Are you crazy? She laughs more than anyone else." He flushed nervously and poked at his glasses.

"Well, what do you expect her to do?" asked Kathy. "Sometimes the only thing anybody can do is laugh, even if we'd all rather slug you, Andy!"

"Oh, that's great! Did she send you here as her great big fierce messenger? Are you her hit man? Pardon me, I mean her hit *person*. Boy, I'm scared to death."

"You just quit it," Kathy said furiously. "I'm not kidding about this. And Marcie doesn't even know I'm talking to you, so you'd better not tell her."

Andy held up his hands. "Okay! Okay! I give up! Just tell me where to go for my execution."

Kathy started walking away, then she turned back. "You aren't a bit funny sometimes, teddy bear."

"What! Teddy bear?"

She left him sputtering in the hall and went to her locker. Marcie was there, waiting for her. "I thought you went to get one of your books?"

"I made a slight detour," said Kathy. "Do you think that people should do what they really want to do?"

"Yeah! Let's do what we really want to do and cut class for the rest of the day and go to the beach for a picnic," Marcie suggested.

"I'm serious. Don't you think that everyone should take a chance just once?"

"I don't know what you're talking about," said Marcie, "but somehow I think I'd rather go to the dentist."

But Kathy was persistent. "If I ask Kevin to the dance, will you ask Andy?"

"You are crazy," Marcie replied flatly. "You've come apart at the seams. Your light bulb went out. Your battery is dead."

"Think about it," said Kathy, and she left Marcie standing in the hall with her mouth open.

"Okay, so I thought about it," Marcie said as they were walking home from school. "I decided that you should be put away someplace so you can't do any damage."

They were passing a yard filled with flowers, and Kathy stopped to study them while Marcie waited impatiently.

"Well?" Marcie demanded finally.

"I'm going to ignore that dumb remark because you aren't yourself today," Kathy replied serenely. "I only proposed that both of us do something we'd really like to do, and maybe it will all turn out fine and we'll have a wonderful time. What do we have to lose?"

Marcie thought hard, scowling. "Well, I don't know what you have to lose, but I'm probably going to lose my life. Andy will kill me."

"No, he won't," Kathy assured her. "Come on. I'm brave enough to try."

Marcie could not resist a challenge. "All right, but if he laughs at me, I'm going to come looking for you."

Kathy smiled grimly. "If he laughs, just tell me."

Marcie scuffed her shoes along the sidewalk. "What if he accepts? Everyone else will laugh. I'm too tall, or he's too short."

Kathy had given this a great deal of thought, for she had been certain that Marcie would bring it up. "What if someone does laugh? I'm not saying that it will happen, but just in case it does, think about me. I'm willing to go to a Port Borden High School dance again, after the last one where everyone got a good look at my panties."

Marcie shouted with laughter. "That wasn't funny!"

"Then why are you laughing?" Kathy asked. "See? You can't help it, because it really was funny. I sure didn't think so at the time, and if anyone but you started laughing, I'd get really mad. But it was funny. Sometimes when I'm all alone and think about it, I start laughing. Or at least I do now. For a long time I cried every time I thought of it."

"You're braver than I am," Marcie said. "I'd still be crying."

"No, you wouldn't. Anyway, I know that it was a lot different from going out with someone who is shorter than you are. I just used it as an example of having the worst thing in the world happen to you. You get over it."

Marcie looked skeptical.

"Going out with Andy *isn't* the worst thing in the world. You're crazy about him," Kathy went on. "So what if you're three inches taller? And so what if someone laughs? Anyway, maybe he grew taller over the winter."

Marcie doubled up with laughter. "Maybe he did," she agreed. "But I probably did, too, so we're right back where we started."

Kathy made a face. "You are impossible," she said. "But now that we have all that over with, is it a deal?"

Marcie walked slower. "I think I'll make a big fool of myself when he turns me down."

"Who would know?" Kathy stopped at the end of her driveway. "If you don't tell, I won't."

Reluctantly, Marcie finally nodded. "Okay. I'll ask him, but I'm not promising when or where. When are you going to ask Kevin?"

"Right now," said Kathy. "Before I lose my nerve. I'm going down to the drugstore and ask him. Just like that."

"Can I come along and watch?" Marcie asked, grinning.

"Only if you don't want to live to be seventeen," Kathy replied firmly. "I'll embarrass myself privately, thanks."

Solemnly, Marcie held a finger to her head and pretended to pull a trigger. Kathy laughed and went into her house.

She left her books in the hall and told her mother that she was going to run an errand downtown. Mrs. Price, engrossed in a book on auto mechanics, looked up and said, "Ummm." Kathy ran before her mother thought to ask what the errand was.

She was not certain she had the courage to do what she

had committed herself to do. She'd be so happy if Kevin agreed to go the the dance with her. But what if he refused?

Oh, I wish the next hour were over with, Kathy thought. Then I'll know one way or the other, and no matter what, at least I tried.

Chapter 17

Kevin was stocking shelves in the beauty department when Kathy entered the drugstore and didn't see her immediately, so she almost lost her nerve. He seemed busy, and there were several people wandering about in the store. Just as she decided to leave, he looked up and saw her.

"What are you doing here?" he asked, surprised.

She laughed nervously. "I was looking for you. I wanted to ask you something."

He put down the box he had been unpacking and stuck his hands in the pockets of his jacket. "You wanted to know what happened to the necklace," he said, grinning. "Someone bought it yesterday, but I didn't find out about it until after school today."

Kathy blinked stupidly. Of course! She had forgotten his concern over selling the necklace. "I'm glad. I'll bet you're relieved," she managed to say.

"I feel lucky, that's for sure," he replied. "Things have been looking up lately. What brought you down here today?"

This is it, Kathy thought, wishing her mouth were not so dry. "I wanted to ask you to the dance," she blurted out.

She panicked when she saw his blank expression. Why did I do it! she raged at herself. I wish I had stayed home and kept my mouth shut.

The terrible silence dragged out until Kathy wanted to die. She wasn't sure whether ten seconds or ten minutes or ten minutes had passed, but she was sure that she had done the wrong thing.

"I'll have to let you know," Kevin said finally. "It's sure nice of you to think about me, though."

Kathy licked her lips nervously. "Well, when you decide, you can call me."

"Sure," he said, and she thought he was deliberately being kind. "I'll call you as soon as I know for certain if I can make it."

Kathy backed away from him, anxious to be gone. "I'll see you later."

She was halfway home before she was aware of her surroundings. He'll say no, she thought, because someone has already asked him. Probably Liz. And now he doesn't know how to tell me. She was embarrassed to the point of tears.

Marcie was right. I must be crazy.

When she arrived home, her mother was in the kitchen, and Kathy asked if she needed any help. Anything to get her mind off Kevin!

"You look like you just lost your last friend," Mrs. Price commented as she finished cutting lettuce for the salad.

"I asked Kevin to the dance," Kathy said unhappily.

"That's nice." Mrs. Price sliced a tomato and didn't look up.

"He said he'd think about it," Kathy went on, and she sat down at the table. "I bet someone else has already asked him."

"There could be a dozen reasons why he said that," her mother said. "After all, he does have a job. Maybe he can't get time off."

Kathy nodded. "Maybe."

She set the table for dinner, and Kathy knew her mother was watching her. As soon as the last napkin was in place, Kathy said, "I guess I'll call Marcie." She was eager to escape from the kitchen and her mother's unspoken sympathy.

Marcie answered the phone and Kathy didn't waste time. "I asked him," she said. "He said he'd think about it."

Kathy could hear Marcie chewing. Finally her friend replied, "Well, that's better than a flat no. At least, that's what it says here in fine print on the bottom of my list of stupid things to tell friends."

"I feel awful," Kathy said simply.

"So do I," said Marcie. "I think I'll go eat a piece of Mom's sponge cake and die."

"Not before you ask Andy!" Kathy cried. "You promised."

"Well, Andy couldn't tell me he needed to think about it because he doesn't think, so I guess he'll just say no."

"I'd settle for a no right now," said Kathy. "Waiting is terrible."

"You know what, Kathy?" Marcie asked. "Everything is terrible. Let me know if you hear anything."

Kathy agreed and hung up. When she went to her room to start her homework, she found that she was unable to concentrate. In her mind's eye, she kept seeing Kevin with Liz at the dance. Or Kevin with anyone but her.

At the dinner table she could only pick at her food, and when the phone rang she expected it to be Marcie or Deb, so Kevin's voice startled her.

"Sorry to take so long to get back to you," he said. "But I had to wait until I saw Dad so I could work out something with him. It's okay. I can go."

"What?" Kathy asked. She was afraid she had not heard him right.

There was a small silence. "I said that I could go to the dance," Kevin said. "That is, if the offer's still open."

"Oh, yes!" exclaimed Kathy. "I mean, of course. I'm so glad you called. Thank you!"

Kevin laughed and she hated herself for babbling, but it was impossible for her to hide her relief. As soon as he hung up, she called Marcie, and when she answered the phone, Kathy shouted, "He said yes! He's going!"

"All right!" Marcie cried. "Spare my eardrums."

"Now it's your turn," Kathy reminded her. "Remember what you promised."

"And I said that I'd pick the time and place, don't forget." Marcie was emphatic. "I'll let you know when the worst is over."

Kathy went to bed happy that night, and she lay awake planning what she would wear to the dance. She was too excited to give much thought to Marcie's plight, other than to wish her luck. But she, Kathy, was through the worst part of it.

By lunchtime the next day, everyone in school seemed to know that Kathy was taking Kevin to the dance, and several girls spoke openly of their envy. Whenever Kathy saw Kevin in the halls, she blushed, but he grinned easily. Nothing seemed to put him off-balance, Kathy thought. But maybe boys were different. She felt like dancing and singing. It was spring, and she had everything she wanted.

Each time Kathy saw Marcie and Andy together, she hoped Marcie was making good use of the opportunity to ask him to the dance, but on the way home that afternoon Marcie said that she hadn't found the courage yet. "I think I'd better get him alone," she added. "That way, when he starts laughing, no one else will hear."

Two days passed, with Marcie dawdling over the problem, and all of Kathy's anxieties were for her friend, until one morning when she found Liz talking to Pris beside the locker.

Kathy did not bother to speak to them, since neither of them ever spoke to her. She bent to take her books from the bottom of the locker, ignoring them, but she was not far enough away to avoid hearing what they were saying.

"So," Liz said, apparently in the middle of an explanation, "he came by last night and apologized about everything, but of course, I understood. What else could he have done about the poor sap. But look, Pris! See what he gave me."

"Oh, it's beautiful!" Kathy heard Pris squeal. "It's like the necklace that was in the jewelry store window."

Kathy froze.

"He made it almost the same, except that there aren't as many leaves. I like it better this way."

Kathy looked up. Liz's fingers toyed with the necklace she wore. A silver necklace, made of tiny leaves connected to a fine chain. It did look almost identical to the one Kevin had left in the store window.

Kathy bent her head and mechanically finished sorting through her books. I have to get away from here, she thought. I'm not going to cry, but I have to get away.

She threw two unwanted books on the bottom of her locker and slammed the door shut.

"Hey!" Pris shouted. "I wasn't done yet!"

Kathy walked away without answering, and Liz and Pris burst out laughing.

Kevin had made a necklace for Liz! He had been planning on going to the dance with her, too. Why had he changed his mind and told Kathy he would go with her? What did they mean when they called her a poor sap?

He hadn't needed time to talk to his father! He had needed time to talk to Liz. But why?

Marcie would know. She knew everything. Kathy could not wait until lunchtime, and she barely listened in her classes. The morning seemed to drag past.

When she was at last seated with Marcie and Deb in the cafeteria, she told them what had happened, and she saw by their expressions that both of them knew what was going on.

"Tell me," she directed them.

Marcie seemed uncomfortable. "I don't believe the story for a minute, but I'll tell you what Liz is saying. She said that Kevin felt sorry for you because he had led you on this last winter, and also, he felt bad about what happened to you at the last dance. So..."

"So I'm his little act of charity, is that it?"

"I told you, I don't believe the story," said Marcie.

"And neither do I" Deb said. "You know Liz. Can you see her letting any boy get away with that? She wouldn't care how bad you felt!"

Kathy shook her head. "No, I can't see her doing something like that. But I can sure see Kevin doing it. He did lead me on last winter. All those times he took me skating! And what about the times I thought he was sharing something special with me when he showed me the jewelry in Mr. Hansen's window? Oh, sure, I can see Kevin telling me he'd go to the dance, and then giving Liz a necklace so she wouldn't feel bad."

She pushed her tray away, unable to eat. "Well, I'll just tell him to forget it. I'm not taking him to the dance."

"Hey, you'd better think it over first," Marcie warned. "Are you sure you want to do that? After all, Deb and I think this is all just another one of Liz's big lies. And Andy thinks so, too."

"Andy!" Kathy cried. "Does everyone in school know?"

Marcie and Deb exchanged glances. "You know how Liz is," Deb said softly.

Kathy's eyes filled with angry tears. "Well, that just does it!" She got up from the table then, and went directly to her next class, where she sat alone in the room and tried to sort out her thoughts until the bell rang and the other students crowded in.

It didn't make any difference whether or not Liz's story were true. Everyone in school believed it, and she wasn't going to go to another dance and be embarrassed.

Kevin still walked her from botany to choir every day, and she took advantage of this to tell him that she would have to take back her invitation. "I'm going away with my folks that weekend," she lied uncomfortably. "Sorry, Kevin, but I'm sure someone else will ask you."

She deliberately walked faster then, cutting in front of him, and she did not hear if he said anything to her. She would not look at him in choir, but instead kept her eyes down, fixed on her music. Eventually the class ended, and Kathy left immediately, not even waiting for Marcie.

Later, sitting on the ground in the middle of her garden, she let herself cry. And when the tears were done, Kathy went back to the house, feeling much older and wiser.

It was, she decided, better not to trust anyone.

A week passed, during which time she refused to discuss the dance with anyone. She had not even asked Marcie if she had yet scraped up enough courage to invite Andy. When Marcie finally told her that she had actually asked him, and that he had accepted, Kathy smiled and said, "Great." But her voice carried no enthusiasm, and she knew that Marcie was hesitant to talk about Andy or the dance with her for fear of reminding her of Kevin.

Her frown was sufficiently obvious to dampen everyone's efforts to talk to her. She concentrated on her studies and walked home in silence with Marcie. In cold fury, she ignored Kevin completely, refusing to walk between classes with him by shaking her head angrily when he approached her. He tried only twice, and then he avoided her cautiously.

Once, when Andy was joking with her, she turned on him and told him to leave her alone. Andy slunk away to confide in Marcie. Kathy had changed, she heard them say, and she didn't care.

It was about time Kathy changed, she thought.

That Saturday, when the air was fragrant with the scents of freshly mowed lawns and salt water, Kathy walked downtown alone, and as she passed the jewelry store, she saw another piece of Kevin's silver jewelry, prominently displayed.

This time he had made a ring, similar to his own, but much smaller. Using the motif of leaves again, he had carved out a delicate design that captivated Kathy. The tiny leaves overlapped slightly, and they were perfect, even to the fragile stems that wound between them.

Mr. Hansen saw her and gestured to her, so she entered the shop. "What do you think?" he cried excitedly. "He's really outdone himself this time."

"It's a beautiful ring," Kathy said sincerely. She wondered if Mr. Hansen knew that she and Kevin were not speaking to each other anymore, and she decided that adults cared very little about what happened in the relationships that were so painful to teenagers.

"It's a little like the one Kevin's grandfather made for him, but much smaller, of course," Mr. Hansen continued. "And I think it's better. He's a fine silversmith, our Kevin."

Mr. Hansen had taken the ring from the window and handed it to Kathy so that she could see it better. Inside the ring she could see Kevin's hallmark, the tiny KW.

"How much is it?" she asked impulsively. She could not bear to think of anyone else wearing the ring. She wanted it for herself, even though she would not be able to wear it to school or anywhere else where someone might recognize it and know who made it. She would not give Kevin and Liz that satisfaction.

The price Mr. Hansen mentioned was nearly as great as the entire amount in Kathy's savings account, but she said, "Save the ring for me, please. I'll pay for it on Monday, if that's all right."

Mr. Hansen was delighted. "But you must try it on first," he insisted. "If it doesn't fit, it can be sized."

Kathy held out her right hand, and when Mr. Hansen slipped the ring on the third finger, she felt an electric thrill, just as she had whenever Kevin touched her.

"It's just a little bit too small," Mr. Hansen said. "But that can be fixed very easily." He took the ring off her finger and put it in a drawer under the counter. "Oh, yes, no problem at all."

If the ring had been too large, Kathy would have told him not to bother sizing it. She would have taken it anyway. But if she could barely get it on her finger, she had better let him fix it, she decided.

He promised her that the ring would be ready on Monday, and Kathy left the shop. She was not sure whether or not she had done the right thing, but she had done what she *wanted* to do. She had to own the ring.

It was the only part of Kevin she would ever have.

Chapter 18

Kathy's parents had gone out to dinner with friends, leaving her home alone that Saturday night, so she made herself popcorn and settled down in front of the television set. The dance was only two weeks away, but she would not let herself think about it. Rather, she concentrated on the following Saturday, when she would be singing in the spring concert. It would be a welcome relief from spending her Saturday nights at home alone, even though she still did not feel very sociable. She didn't mind being around people, but she didn't feel like talking very often. There wouldn't be much talk at the concert. The choir members would be too nervous.

When the phone rang, she expected it to be Marcie again. Earlier in the day, Marcie had reported that Andy had asked her to go to a movie with him, so that they could practice being civilized before the dance. That was Andy's excuse, Marcie had explained, but she was willing, no matter what the reason. "I guess we do need the practice," she had concluded.

Marcie was probably getting cold feet and needed encouragement, Kathy thought as she walked to the phone.

Kevin did not wait for formalities. "I'm coming over to see you," he said abruptly. "At nine o'clock. You wait on the porch for me."

Kathy gripped the phone. "What are you talking about?" she demanded.

"I'll tell you when I get there. You be waiting for me at

nine. I'll take you for a short drive, and we're going to get something straightened out."

Kathy hung up on him. How dare he call her and issue orders? He was bad enough when he was being disgustingly kind. She would not tolerate his temper tantrums.

At nine o'clock she heard his car stop in front and she deliberately raised the volume on the television set. Kevin knocked on the door, but Kathy sat stubbornly in front of the TV.

Kevin knocked again, louder this time. "I know your folks aren't home," he shouted. "Their car is gone." He knocked even louder. "I'll keep knocking until your neighbors complain," he threatened.

Kathy went to the door, furious, and yanked it open. "How dare you threaten me!" she cried.

Kevin stepped inside and shut the door behind him. "I don't like acting this way," he said, "but you don't leave a guy any choice. You are the most stubborn, stuck-up—"

"Stuck-up!" Kathy shouted, remembering her first painful days at school when everyone had thought she was a snob. "I am not stuck-up!"

"Oh, no?" Kevin asked. "Why won't you walk to class with me? You'd rather walk by yourself than with me. Liz said you told everyone that."

"Liz!" Kathy shouted. "Don't say one word about her! All she ever does is lie, and I don't want to hear it."

"Well, if you know that much about her, then why did you believe what she said about the necklace? I heard about that fairy tale she's been spreading. You *must* have believed it!"

"What?" Kathy backed up, astonished. "What are you talking about?"

"You couldn't ask me about it, could you? You just had to swallow the first stupid story you heard. Liz's parents asked me months ago to make a necklace like the one I left in Mr. Hansen's window. They wanted to give it to her for her birthday. I was going to use the money I got to take you to the senior prom."

Kathy sat down, numb. Kevin moved closer, towering over her.

"I know you bought the ring I left in the store this week, and I came here to tell you that it isn't for sale, not to you, anyway." Kevin's face was tight with anger, and Kathy was astonished by his emotion. "When Mr. Hansen called me and asked me to size the ring, he told me you were the one who wanted it. So I picked it up just before he closed the store." Kevin reached in his pocket and pulled out the ring, showing it to her. "I won't let you buy it, Kathy. Not this ring!"

Angrily, Kathy got to her feet. "I'm buying it and it's mine. I'm not going to put up with anything else from you, Kevin Wade. You just make me sick! First you tell me you're going to go to the dance with me, and then I find out that you were only feeling sorry for me. You just get out of here right now, but leave that ring here! It's mine!"

"It was going to be yours!" Kevin shouted. "I made it for you, and I was going to give it to you before you even asked me to the dance. Then, when you said you didn't want to take me, I put it in the store. It sure didn't seem like you'd ever be wearing it. And if I can't *give* it to you, you aren't going to have it." He put the ring back in his pocket and started for the door. "Now you know the truth."

Kathy watched him walk toward the door, and she was struggling to understand everything that he had said. Nothing made sense, and he couldn't go until she understood!

"Wait!" she cried. "I don't understand any of this. What do you mean, you were going to give the ring to me? Why would you do something like that?"

"Not because I feel sorry for you, Kathy," he replied, and his face told her that he was still angry. "Why do you think I would give you a ring? It's because I really like you. I wanted us to go steady, do you understand? And not just this year, either. For as long as you wanted."

Kathy clasped her hands to keep them from shaking. "Why didn't you tell me that you were making a necklace for Liz's parents to give her?" she asked. Her gray eyes sparked with anger. "You know what she's like! She makes things up all the time."

"And you don't think things through," he said in retaliation. "This wouldn't have happened if you hadn't jumped to conclusions."

It was true, she thought. That was what she had done, more than once where he was concerned. Miserably, she turned away and sat down again. "Okay, I guess you're right," she conceded. "Liz has always been a big pain for me, and I let her get to me, even when I shouldn't. It's not that I haven't tried to ignore her. But I guess I just couldn't."

"And you wouldn't let me talk to you," said Kevin, making sure she got the point. "I could have explained, if you hadn't been so stubborn."

He still sounded angry, and she decided abruptly that the whole thing was hopeless. "Okay. I understand. Now just leave me alone," she said.

"My pleasure," he replied bitterly. Kathy looked down at her lap, and she heard the door slam. She squeezed her eyes shut, hoping to control her tears, but they spurted between her eyelids anyway.

"Marcie was right," she muttered aloud. "Everything is awful."

"It doesn't have to be awful," Kevin said from the hall. "We could change it."

Kathy's eyes popped open. He hadn't left! He was leaning against the front door.

"Too much has gone wrong," Kathy blurted stubbornly.

Kevin walked back into the living room and sat down next to her. "Nothing is wrong that we can't fix. Please, Kathy, try to be a little more realistic. You can tell if things make sense or not."

Kathy turned her face away from him. "It all made sense to me."

"Only because you listened to everybody else. You never gave me a chance."

"Look who's talking! You listened to Liz's lies!"

Kevin bit his lip. "You're right. I did listen. But the way you acted sometimes..."

"The way I acted!"

"Okay. I was wrong, too. But if we just talk to each other..."

Kathy's hands were folded tightly in her lap. She stared down at them through hot tears, wanting to believe him more than she had ever wanted anything.

She felt Kevin's arm slip around her, pulling her close to his chest. "I'd like us to have a new start," he said softly. "Let's promise each other something. We won't believe anything about each other until we check it out. And with each other, not with friends who mean well but might not know the truth."

Kathy raised her tear-stained face and Kevin cupped her chin in one of his hands. "Promise?" he whispered.

She nodded, and then he kissed her. Oh, she believed him now!

Kevin pulled away from her for a moment, and he seemed shaken. "Can you imagine how different things would have been if I hadn't believed that you were interested in Andy and Gordon, and if you hadn't believed that I wanted Liz?" He laughed a little, and before he kissed her again, he said, "I guess I'd better follow my own advice. I wanted this to happen the first time I saw you."

He pulled her to her feet. "I can't stay," he said. "I don't want to get your folks upset at me. But if you're not busy tomorrow, we could go on a picnic."

"That sounds wonderful."

"And you'll get the ring then," he promised. "I can size it tonight."

She raised her face for one more kiss, hoping that it told him everything he wanted to know, and when he left she whirled around the living room, laughing aloud. It was going to be all right after all!

Chapter 19

Kathy waited to tell Marcie about the ring until she and her friend walked to school on Monday morning. Marcie grasped Kathy's hand and marveled over it. "I'm so glad for you," she said. "I was afraid that you were silly enough to throw Kevin away."

"We talked things over," Kathy told her. "And everything is fine now. It's going to stay that way, too. How about you and Andy? Did you have a good time at the movie?"

Marcie blushed. "The movie was fine."

Kathy looked at her curiously. "So what's wrong, then?"

Marcie looked down at her feet. "If you laugh, I'll murder you right here."

"Then I'll be careful not to laugh," Kathy assured her. "Tell me."

"When we got home after the movie," Marcie began, and then she started laughing helplessly. Kathy waited until Marcie had control of herself and could begin again. "When he took me home," Marcie gasped, "he asked me to stand on the sidewalk, and then he got up on the first porch step and kissed me good night."

Kathy stared at her, trying to control her laughter, but Marcie's own sparkling eyes made that impossible. "Admit it," Marcie said. "It's the most unromantic thing you ever heard."

"Not quite," replied Kathy. "The most unromantic thing would be if he hadn't kissed you at all."

"I suppose." Marcie sighed. "But somehow I don't think this relationship is going very far."

"I hope it goes far enough for the two of you to double-date with us on the night of the dance," Kathy said. She and Kevin had decided the day before that they wanted the comic couple with them.

"Absolutely," Marcie declared. "And let's go somewhere before the dance where we can have a really big dinner."

Ten minutes before first bell, they were strolling toward the hall where their lockers were located. The whole school looked different to Kathy today. Depressed and lonely for so long, she had nearly forgotten what the place was really like. The gray, sad world she had thought awaited her within the old building was gone. Students jostled and laughed in the hall, and their smiles often included her. Even their clothes seemed more brightly colored.

"I don't know if it's spring or just me," Marcie said, "but doesn't this place look halfway bearable today?"

"That's what I was thinking," Kathy responded, grinning. "It's marvelous what a nice weekend can do for our mental states."

"Hmm," Marcie mused. "I wonder what we're having for lunch."

"Marcie!" Andy bawled from behind them. "Where are the drama club recruitment posters? You said you'd put them up."

"I did not!" Marcie retaliated instantly.

Andy was furiously hopping around both the girls. "Oh, yes, you did! How am I supposed to sign up new members for next year if you don't even put up the posters? Admit it! You didn't even finish them!"

"I did, too!" Marcie shouted.

Andy suddenly calmed down and peered at her through his glasses. "I've got an idea. You'd be great in the drama club." He circled the tall girl happily. "What do you think,

Kathy? Can't you see her as Juliet, leaning over the balcony?"

Marcie scowled at him. "You want to live until lunchtime, you little crackpot? Forget it."

But Andy took her by the hand. "Marcie, my love, come away with me to the stairwell and let me persuade you."

Marcie laughed helplessly and followed him, calling back to Kathy to wait for her at her locker. Grinning, Kathy made her way through the students who had paused to enjoy another of the arguments for which Marcie and Andy had become famous.

"Hey, Kathy."

Kathy looked back, startled to hear Liz call her name. Standing with a group of her friends, Liz beckoned and smiled.

But Kathy approached cautiously. She knew Liz hadn't suddenly become friendly, so what did she want?

Liz touched the silver necklace she wore. "You never told me how you liked my necklace," she said, and her smile turned wicked. Pris, standing on one side of her, snickered.

Kathy's face burned. Idiot! she told herself. Won't you ever learn? "The necklace is beautiful," she replied quietly, longing to show Liz her ring but knowing better than to risk a scene.

But Liz would not be put off. "Kevin said that it has a very special meaning," she smirked.

Liz was at it again! But before Kathy could reply, the girl standing behind Pris pushed forward and cried, "Stop it!"

It was the plump girl with the long black hair who had said, "Hey, frog princess!" to Kathy and then had congratulated her for doing well at the music festival. "Why don't you leave Kathy alone, Liz? She's never done anything to you."

Pris gasped, but Liz's eyes narrowed dangerously. "You'd better look out, Jennifer. I'm not going to forget this."

Defiantly, Jennifer turned to Kathy. "We'd better get to

our lockers. It's almost time for the bell." And to Kathy's astonishment, the girl slipped her arm through hers. "Come on," she whispered, "before she throws something."

Kathy looked back once, to see Liz staring after them, her face red with anger. Pris was gabbling nervously.

"Is she coming after us?" Jennifer asked.

Kathy shook her head, and Jennifer relaxed. "Oh, boy," she said with a sigh. "I've wanted to do that for a long time. Liz can be an absolute creep. And people go along with her because she has such a nasty temper." They had reached the safety of the hall where the lockers were. "Why don't we do something after school sometime?" Jennifer asked. "If you want to, that is."

Kathy could not have stopped smiling if the roof had fallen on her. "Yes. We could do something after school. That would be fun."

Both of them rushed to their lockers then, for time was running out, and Marcie walked up to Kathy, wide-eyed.

"Do I dare believe my eyes? Has someone else deserted Liz?"

Kathy laughed as the bell rang and tugged open her locker. "Tell you at lunch. It'll take me that long to believe it." She grabbed her books, slammed the locker door, and ran. I belong here, she thought. I really belong here.

Chapter 20

The dance was being held in the school gym, and once again Marcie and her fellow art students had done a beautiful job of decorating. Kathy stopped Kevin in the doorway and said, "Just a minute. I want to see it all from here."

Marcie had used spring flowers for a theme this time, and the room was blooming with them. Every place she could, she had put armloads of apple and cherry blossoms, too.

Kathy saw the tulips that she had donated from her garden. Marcie had given them a place of honor, at the senior class president's table, and Kathy was pleased.

"It looks great," Kevin said. "Marcie must have worked hard on this."

"She was up here all day," Kathy told him. "Come on, let's find our places."

Kevin was wearing his dark-blue suit again, and he already had traces of a tan, so Kathy thought that he looked gorgeous. She was wearing a short dress made of a thin white fabric with a bright-pink silk scarf tied around her waist. Marcie had made her a small wreath of apple blossoms which she wore pressed down over her blond curls, and she knew from the light in Kevin's eyes that she looked pretty.

Marcie and Andy came in behind them, arguing noisily. "I'm telling you, you're wrong!" Marcie declared. "You can too form another band, and it will be cheaper for us at the next Beaux Arts Ball. You'll give me a discount, of course."

"Listen to the woman!" Andy implored. "She's already planning for a dance that won't happen until our senior year. She never quits!"

"You need time to train some new musicians," Marcie said defensively. "At the rate you're going, all you'll have are three boys who can't read music and that disgusting guy who blows on a jug!"

"Cal is a musical genius!" Andy howled. "You can't put him down!"

They wandered away to find their places at one of the tables, still bickering companionably, and Kevin and Kathy both laughed.

"That's a match made in heaven," he said, and he took her hand.

And so are we, she thought happily.

The music was wonderful, they agreed, although Andy's band had been better, and as soon as they located their place cards, Kathy and Kevin turned to the dance floor. Kevin's arm slid around her, and they enjoyed one set of slow music before returning to their seats. By that time, Tom and Deb had arrived and shared their table with them for a while before they joined in the dancing.

"It's more crowded than I thought it would be," Kevin said. He straightened the apple blossom wreath in Kathy's hair and smiled down at her affectionately.

"Every ticket was sold," she told him, not adding that Marcie had told her that Liz had been unable to buy a ticket when she'd finally given up and asked Gordon to go with her.

They lingered at the table alone through most of the evening, even though they both enjoyed dancing. Kathy felt like she would never get tired of listening to Kevin.

"What are you thinking about, right this minute?" Kevin asked.

"I was thinking about how nice this is," she said.

Kevin leaned close to her. "Did I tell you how good you look?"

"Only about a hundred times so far," she replied calmly. "But don't let that stop you from telling me again."

He laughed. "If you don't watch out, you'll end up with a swelled head."

She looked up at him and grinned. Her face flushed with color. "Is that any way to talk to your best girl, Kevin Wade?"

"No, it isn't. There's only one way I want to talk to my best girl right now." With that, Kevin pulled Kathy close to him and kissed her.

"That's the kind of talking we should do more often," Kathy said.

When a teen looks for romance, she's looking for

CAPRICE

	Title	Code / Price
____	**A NEW LOVE FOR LISA**	57169-7/ $1.95
____	**PRESCRIPTION FOR LOVE**	67771-1/ $2.25
____	**PROGRAMMED FOR LOVE**	68250-2/ $1.95
____	**SING A SONG OF LOVE**	76726-5/ $1.95
____	**SOMEONE FOR SARA**	77461-X/ $1.95
____	**A SPECIAL LOVE**	77788-0/ $1.95
____	**STARDUST SUMMER**	78052-0/ $1.95
____	**SUNRISE**	16981-9/ $1.95
____	**SURFER GIRL**	79101-8/ $1.95
____	**S.W.A.K. SEALED WITH A KISS**	79115-8/ $1.95
____	**THREE'S A CROWD**	16921-5/ $1.95
____	**TOMMY LOVES TINA**	81649-5/ $1.95
____	**TOO YOUNG TO KNOW**	81715-7/ $1.95
____	**TWO LOVES FOR TINA**	83380-2/ $1.95
____	**WHEN WISHES COME TRUE**	88258-7/ $1.95
____	**WISH FOR TOMORROW**	89446-1/ $1.95

Prices may be slightly higher in Canada.

Available at your local bookstore or return this form to:

TEMPO
Book Mailing Service
P.O. Box 690, Rockville Centre, NY 11571

Please send me the titles checked above. I enclose _____ Include 75¢ for postage and handling if one book is ordered; 25¢ per book for two or more not to exceed $1.75. California, Illinois, New York and Tennessee residents please add sales tax.

NAME_____

ADDRESS_____

CITY_____ STATE/ZIP_____

(allow six weeks for delivery)   T10/b

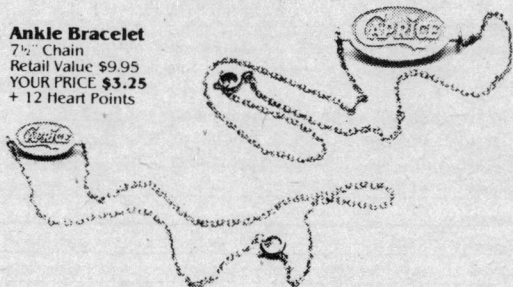